ઌ৵ঙ৩ঌ৵

THE SECRET

OF THE

LONELY

GRAVE

ৎ৩ঙ৵ঌ

Best wishes,
Albert Bell

ఈ సురు ళ

OTHER BOOKS BY
ALBERT A. BELL, JR

CONTEMPORARY FICTION:

DEATH GOES DUTCH
KILL HER AGAIN

HISTORICAL FICTION:

ALL ROADS LEAD TO MURDER
DAUGHTER OF LAZARUS

NONFICTION

PERFECT GAME, IMPERFECT LIVES:
*A MEMOIR CELEBRATING THE
50TH ANNIVERSARY OF DON LARSEN'S PERFECT GAME*

EXPLORING THE
NEW TESTAMENT WORLD

CO-AUTHORED WITH JAMES B. ALLIS:

RESOURCES IN ANCIENT PHILOSOPHY

ఈ సురు ళ

THE SECRET

OF THE

LONELY

GRAVE

❧ ❦ ❧

ALBERT A. BELL, JR

CLAYSTONE BOOKS

BOONE, NORTH CAROLINA
2007

A Claystone Book

from
INGALLS PUBLISHING GROUP, INC
197 New Market Center, #135
Boone, NC 28607
www.ingallspublishinggroup.com

Cover concept by Steven Beckwith
Cover design by Ann Thompson Nemcosky
Text design by schuyler kaufman

ISBN: 978-1-932158-79-3
Library of Congress Catalog Number 2007922580

Revised printing: 2007

10 9 8 7 6 5 4 3 2

Printed in the United States of America

For my
Children

and my
Grandson

Author's Note

This story is fiction, but it has a real setting. It's set in southern Kentucky, a few miles from the Tennessee state line, in an area known as the Land Between the Lakes. Barkley Lake and Kentucky Lake were created in the 1940s and 1950s when the government built dams to control flooding on the Tennessee and Cumberland Rivers. The town of Cadiz is the largest town close to the lakes. Children from all over the area go to school there, in the Trigg County Elementary and Middle Schools.

For a number of years my wife's family owned a houseboat on Lake Barkley She and her parents and our children enjoyed fishing. I did not, so I used to find other ways to spend my time. One day I walked through an old cemetery near the lake. I was surprised to see one tombstone set off by itself. I began to wonder why somebody would be buried apart from the others that way. That was the beginning of this story.

There are some quotations from an old diary in the story. Some of those were taken from a diary written by a member of my wife's family right after the Civil War.

There are a number of people I need to thank. Members of two writers' groups to which I belong have read and made comments on different chapters. Their help has been extremely valuable. Crystal Hancock and her class at Trigg County Elementary School read an earlier version of the book and invited me down to speak to them. It was a lot of fun and they gave me some ideas for a sequel, which I do hope to write before too long. Fifth-grade classes at Sylvan Christian Elementary School in Grand Rapids, Michigan, also invited me to speak and gave me a set of drawings they had made based on the book.

❧ ❦ ❧

THE SECRET

OF THE

LONELY GRAVE

CHAPTER 1

THE SCHOOL BUS jerked to a stop, the next-to-last stop on the route. Kendra and I picked up our backpacks. At least I didn't have to worry about getting past Dwayne Mitchell this time. Whenever I walk past Dwayne's seat, he kicks me or tries to trip me. But today Kendra and I ran to the bus after school and got seats near the front.

She and I jumped down from the bottom step and the door whooshed shut behind us. As the bus pulled away, Dwayne stuck his head out a window and made a 'woo-o-o-ooh' noise, like a ghost.

"Go soak your head, Dwayne!" I yelled at the bus's tail lights.

"That was clever, Steve, real clever," Kendra said. "He can't hear you now."

"That's why I didn't waste one of my good lines on him."

She slung her backpack onto her shoulder. "The last time you gave him one of your 'good lines,' didn't he punch your face in?"

I didn't say anything, just picked up my backpack and started up the road that leads past the cemetery and the church to our homes at the top of the hill. The hill isn't really steep, but the walk seems longer on a hot day like this.

"I'm sorry," Kendra said as she caught up with me. "I know Dwayne gives you a hard time. I shouldn't make it worse."

"I don't see why he's always picking on me! I never did anything to him."

"Dwayne's just a jerk. School will be out in a week. You won't have to worry about him this summer."

"He lives close enough, I bet he'll be around."

"Maybe not. Most kids don't want to hang around here because of the cemetery."

"Dwayne's not most kids."

Dwayne had made that ghost noise because most of our friends consider it scary to walk past a cemetery. Kendra and I don't just walk past the cemetery, we walk through it. For me that's not as scary as walking past Dwayne on the bus. Nobody in the cemetery has ever kicked me.

"Have you finished that story you were writing about him?" Kendra asked. "The one you showed me Saturday."

"Yeah. I'll print off a copy and bring it over."

I like to write stories. Next to baseball, it's what I like best. In this story, Dwayne and I were on opposite teams. I was playing second base, my favorite position. Earlier in the game he had slid into me and cut my hand, but I stayed in the game. Now it was the top of the ninth, a tie game, and the bases were loaded, with two out. Dwayne came to bat. He hit a line drive. I leaped and caught it! Then my team scored in the bottom of the ninth and won the game.

"Are you going to send this one to the newspaper? Everybody liked that story you wrote back in March, that they published on the kids' page."

"I don't think I'll send this one. Dwayne wouldn't like it."

"Who cares what Dwayne thinks? It's a good story. Just change the names."

"Yeah, I could do that."

I looked across the road at the tourist cottages next to Philips' Grocery Store, the way I always do. My mom and dad owned those cottages. But then they got divorced, when I was five. They aren't fancy, just square little buildings set in a U-shape around the office and a swimming pool. Mom tried to brighten them up by painting each door a different color and calling them the 'Rainbow Cottages.' The next owner kept the name. They look shabby compared to the new motels that have opened around here recently. But they're cheaper than the motels.

I wish there was some other way to get to the top of the hill. It's been six years since the divorce, but every time I look at those cottages I remember my dad teaching me to swim in that pool, or playing ball with me in front of the office.

We were a regular family then. Like the couple sitting by the pool now while their kids played in the water. The father looked up and followed Kendra and me with his eyes.

We get this reaction from strangers a lot. I've tried to write a story about it. Some people can't seem to understand that an African-American girl and a white boy can be friends. We've been neighbors for six years and friends for one day less than that.

I forgot about the man by the pool when a bulldozer roared farther up the hill.

"Somebody's starting on another house," Kendra said.

"Aw, man, that's the last open lot on this side of the road. I wonder if we'll ever see the lake again."

"Maybe some kids our age will move in." Kendra always thinks things are going to turn out good.

"They'll probably be friends of Dwayne's," I said.

Until last summer we were able to climb down the hill on that side of the road and go swimming in the lake. But then old Mrs. Bradford died. As long as anybody could remember, she lived in a big house at the top of the hill, and she owned all the land down to the 'Rainbow Cottages.' Her land had been divided into lots and sold. Her old house had been for sale since school started. It looked more run-down and spookier every day.

This part of western Kentucky is becoming a popular vacation area. That's good, my mom says, because it means tourist money coming in. But it also means people like us, who've lived around the lake all our lives, are being cut off from it because we can't afford lake-front property.

Kendra and I walked up the hill in silence. She's eleven, like me, but tall for her age. I'm four months younger and three inches shorter than she is. At first we played together because there weren't any other kids our age in the neighborhood. Now we do stuff together just because we like each other. My mom is assistant manager of a hardware store, so I stay at Kendra's house, across the street from mine, for the two hours between the end of school and the time my mom gets home.

We usually have a good time, but lately Kendra's started treating me like a little brother. My mom keeps telling me girls start their growth spurt earlier than boys do. "You'll catch up with her pretty soon," she says. That doesn't make me feel any better, because I know my dad is short, unless he's taken a growth spurt since the last time I saw him, two years ago.

What really bothers me is that Kendra and I don't always want to do the same things now. We used to play board games and cards. Now she takes piano lessons and plays tennis. She won the first tournament she played in last month. And she likes to read dumb mystery stories. I like playing baseball, or watching baseball on TV, or reading and writing about it, and organizing my baseball card collection.

Kendra's also getting more sensitive about being black. During Black History Month we studied slavery and the Civil War in school. She got really angry about how African slaves were treated. She almost cried in class when she gave her report about the Underground Railroad that helped slaves escape. She showed us reward posters for them on the internet. 'They were treated like criminals,' she said.

But she and I still hang out together.

When we're walking down the hill in the morning and back up in the afternoon we go by her sister's grave. Her sister died three years ago. She was at a party at another girl's house and drowned in the swimming pool. Her name was Moniqa and she was six when it happened. Kendra stops by the grave for a minute every morning and every afternoon.

There's another grave that we look at every day, too. We call it the 'lonely grave.' It sits by itself all the way at the lower end of the cemetery, ten yards or so from the other graves and close to a hedge that runs beside the cemetery. It looks pretty old. We've never gone over to see who's buried there, but we always look at it. Sometimes we try to guess why somebody would be buried all alone like that.

Kendra says I ought to write a story about it. But the stories I write always start with something I know, like baseball. How could I write a story about somebody who died—maybe a long time ago—when I don't know anything about them?

Kendra grabbed my arm. "Steve, look! There are flowers on the lonely grave."

[*Note: The texts of some reward posters can be found, beginning on page 157*]

CHAPTER 2

"FLOWERS ON THE grave? So what?" I said. "People put flowers on graves all the time."

Kendra's always trying to make ordinary things seem mysterious. If she sees a strange car in front of a house on our street, she writes down the license number. 'The police might need it later,' is what she always says.

"Not on *that* grave," she said. "Nobody puts flowers on that one. We've walked by here since first grade, and we've never seen flowers on it. Why would somebody put them there now?"

"I don't care. I just want to get home and get something to eat. Lunch was *awful* today. They must be cleaning out the freezers before school's out."

"But this is mysterious," Kendra protested.

"You read too many kid detective books."

"Well, *I* want to know why those flowers are there." I knew that tone of voice. She had her mind made up.

"Hey, where are you going?"

"To look at the evidence," Kendra said over her shoulder as she crossed the shallow ditch beside the road and climbed the low bank up to the cemetery.

"What evidence?"

"The flowers. Come on! You're not scared, are you?"

I wasn't scared. I just didn't think it was any of our business. And I *was* hungry. But if Kendra went and I didn't, she'd never let me hear the end of it.

Kendra slowed down and dropped her backpack as she approached the grave. I caught up with her and dropped my backpack beside hers.

"They're wildflowers," she said. "Like the ones in the field over there."

A hedge along the back of the cemetery separated it from an unplowed field with all kinds of weeds and flowers growing in it. The flowers on the grave were set in a small plastic foam bucket with a sponge in the bottom.

"That's one of the bait buckets from Philips' store," I said.

The grave-stone was about three feet high, a rectangle chiseled to a point on top. Wind and rain had worn the edges and the letters, but we could still read what it said:

AMANDA ALLEN
BELOVED DAUGHTER OF
MATTHEW AND LAURA ALLEN
BORN JUNE 10, 1856
DIED OCT 12, 1862

"Gosh, she was only six years old," Kendra said sadly, "just like Moniqa."

"Why would anybody put flowers on a little girl's grave when she's been dead for that long?"

"It is mysterious, like I said. Nobody would just walk along the road, see the grave, and suddenly decide to pick some flowers."

"Yeah. They must have been in the cemetery and noticed this grave." I glanced over my shoulder, just in case the somebody was still around.

"But why were they here? And why put flowers on this grave and none of the others?"

"I don't know, but somebody wanted the flowers to last for a while. They walked over to Philips' store and bought this bucket and the sponge. Were they here this morning when we came down to catch the bus?" I couldn't remember.

"I didn't notice. But we were late—you couldn't find your precious baseball glove—so we were in a hurry. I don't think I even looked over here."

I glanced around, liking this place less and less. "We don't know who put them here, or why, and I want to go home. I'm hungry."

"Okay," Kendra said. "I don't think we can learn any more about the case right now anyway."

"Stop playing detective! There isn't a 'case.' Real kids don't solve mysteries."

"You're just jealous because you didn't see them first." Kendra crossed her arms and lifted her nose in the air. "If we don't know who put the flowers here, or why, then it's a mystery. That's what a mystery *is*, not knowing who did something or why."

༻ ৎৎ ৪৩ ৎৎ ༺

The next morning, after we stopped by Moniqa's grave, we checked for new 'evidence' at the lonely grave. But the flowers looked just like they had the afternoon before. The grave was under the shadow of a big tree, so the sun couldn't dry them out.

But on Wednesday morning there was a new batch of flowers, with a few pieces of greenery stuck in. Kendra and I had left for the bus stop a few minutes early so we would have time to check out anything unusual. We ran over to the grave.

Kendra suddenly put her arm out to stop me a few feet away from the flowers. "Don't mess up any footprints."

"Footprints? What footprints?"

"Let's look around. There might be some."

"It hasn't rained in almost two weeks, Kendra. The ground's as hard as artificial turf on a baseball field. Nobody can make footprints on it."

She walked around, bent over, looking for footprints anyway. "Okay, I guess there aren't any. So, what do we know so far?" She got ready to itemize things on her fingers. It's a habit of hers that really bugs me. "First, the old flowers were still here yesterday afternoon. Second, the new flowers were here before"—she checked her watch—"seven-forty-five. That means somebody switched them during that time."

"Probably this morning," I said as I knelt by the little bucket of flowers.

"Why do you say that?" Kendra asked. She was ready to go on to the next finger but couldn't seem to think of anything to itemize on it.

"Because there's still some water on the side of the bucket and on the ground around it, like somebody spilled it just a little while ago."

"Very good!" Kendra patted me on the shoulder. "I'll make a detective out of you yet."

I couldn't admit it to her, but this whole business suddenly seemed a lot more interesting. Somebody had been here, maybe just a few minutes ago. Who? Why? It was actually kind of scary. I walked around the tombstone, looking for anything that might have been disturbed or something that might have been dropped. When I got to the back side of the marker I studied it more closely, then dropped to one knee and ran my hand over the stone.

"What is it?" Kendra asked. "What do you see?"

"I'm not sure. I think there's something carved on the back, some kind of shape, but you can barely make it out now."

Kendra knelt beside me. "Yeah, I see it. Something round with something sticking out of it."

"It looks like a person's hand," I said. "You know, when you make a fist and point at something."

"Are you sure?" Kendra said. "I don't see any lines to make the folded-up fingers. And why would somebody put a pointing hand on the back of a tombstone?"

"It's not carved as deep as the letters on the other side. Maybe it wasn't even done by the person who made the tombstone. Kids could have done it." I got out the little notebook and pencil I always carry with me and made a sketch of the design, as best I could see it.

"I wish I had a magnifying glass," I said.

Just then the school bus rumbled around the curve and slowed down for our stop.

"Oh, rats!" Kendra cried. "Just when we're getting somewhere. I wish we could skip school and figure this out."

But I was already running toward the bus. "You can sit here all day if you want to," I called over my shoulder. "We're playing the third game of the school World Series today at recess!"

⊷⟨∝ℬ∾⟩⊶

There weren't any new flowers on the lonely grave Thursday morning. Kendra told me she hadn't expected to find any.

"There's a pattern developing, see?" she said, ticking things off on her fingers again. "Monday, flowers. Tuesday, the same flowers. Wednesday, new flowers. Thursday, the same flowers. Friday ...?" She tapped her little finger with the index finger of the other hand. "Wanna make a bet?"

Friday morning we found fresh flowers, but again no clues. While we waited for the bus, we traded guesses about who might be bringing the flowers and why so early in the morning.

"I'll bet it's somebody so creepy she doesn't want to be seen," I said. "Like on 'Creature Feature' on Saturday afternoon. Some old, old lady in a black dress with a veil to cover her deformed face." I scrunched my face up and began to lurch toward Kendra, cackling like a witch.

"Cut it out!" Kendra squealed. "People like that aren't real. This is probably a perfectly normal person who—"

"Who creeps around at night leaving flowers on the grave of some little girl she doesn't even know. Yeah, that's perfectly normal."

"Maybe she *does* know her," Kendra said, "or knows something about her. Maybe she comes from the same family."

"How could that be? Amanda didn't have any children. She was just a kid when she died."

"Maybe she had brothers or sisters, like Moniqa and me. You know, this is kind of like something I read about on the internet. Somebody leaves flowers on Edgar Allan Poe's grave every year on his birthday. Nobody knows who it is."

"That's weird, but I can kind of understand it. Poe's a famous writer, and he wrote some creepy stories. But why would somebody leave flowers on a little girl's grave way out here? What kind of freak is she?"

"A Flower Freak," Kendra said. "Hey, we've been talking about a woman, but the Flower Freak could be a man."

"A man!" I snorted, picking up my backpack and glove. "Why do you think a *man* would be doing this?"

Kendra put a hand on her hip, just like her mother does when she's ticked off. "He might be a very nice man. He might be related to her family or something. We just don't know," she said sadly. "We don't know anything."

"I know how we might find out something. Right now."

"How?"

"Come on. We've got a couple of minutes before the bus gets here."

With Kendra pleading for me to tell her what I had in mind, I led the way to Philips' store, which opens at six-thirty every morning. I was glad to see Mrs. Philips and not her son behind the counter. Her son just considers us a nuisance. He won't allow more than two kids at a time in the store. But Mrs. Philips is

nice. If you could design your own grandmother, she would be
Mrs. Philips, except for the yellow teeth and the cigarette breath.
She knows all the kids around here.

"Good morning, Steve, Kendra," Mrs. Philips said with a
smile. "What can I do for you?"

"Could you tell us if somebody bought one of your small
bait buckets Monday morning?" I asked.

"Oh, hon, this time of year we sell a dozen of those things
every day," Mrs. Philips said. She laughed a little bit, with a
rattling kind of noise in her chest.

"Empty ones?"

Mrs. Philips nodded. "Sure, empty ones too. They're just the
right size for keeping a couple of canned drinks cold in ice."

The school bus's brakes screeched. "Well, thanks anyway,"
I said, and Kendra and I turned for the door.

"I'm getting in some new baseball cards this afternoon,
Steve!" Mrs. Philips called after us.

⋖ ⊘⊗⊘ ⋗

When we came to church on Sunday morning we didn't know
what to expect. Would the Flower Freak take the weekend
off? Or would the pattern of fresh flowers every other day
continue?

We couldn't see the grave from the church, which is almost
at the top of the hill. The service seemed even longer than usual.
When it was finally over, we slipped off to check the lonely
grave while our parents talked with friends. The flowers that had
been there Friday were wilting in the heat.

"Well, what would Nancy Drew think about this?" I said. It
really irritates Kendra for me to make fun of what she reads.

Before she could answer, her mother called from the top
of the hill. "What on earth are you two doing down there?" she
asked when we had run back up the hill to her. "I've been looking
all over for you."

"We were just ... walking around," Kendra said. She gave
me a look that warned me not to say anything more.

But her mother knew us too well. "What were you up to,
Kendra Louise? It's not like you to hide things from me."

"We were looking at some flowers," I said. The glare I got
from Kendra promised trouble later.

Mrs. Jordan craned her neck to see. "What flowers? Are you messing with something?"

"No, ma'am. The flowers on that grave way down there." I pointed. "The one off by itself."

"What's so special about that grave?" Mrs. Jordan asked.

"It's a little girl's grave, from 1862," Kendra said, "We don't know why somebody's started putting flowers on it."

"That is odd," Mrs. Jordan admitted. "There might be an easy way to solve your little mystery, though."

"How?" we both asked. Kendra looked disappointed. I knew it wasn't a 'little' mystery to her, and she didn't want somebody to solve it for her. I wanted to get this business cleared up right away so we could get on to more important things. It was summer. There had to be more important things.

"You might ask Reverend Grant if he knows anything about it," Kendra's mother said. "Why don't we do that now? Everybody else has left."

We followed her back to the steps of the church where Mr. Jordan, my mom, and my Gramma and Grampa Patterson were talking to the pastor. When we explained why we were interested in the grave, Gramma Patterson looked at me funny.

"Don't you children have anything better to do than poke around a cemetery?" she said before anyone else could speak. "If it's flowers you want, come over to my house. You can pull the weeds out of mine."

Reverend Grant didn't know anything about the flowers. "I know hardly anything about that old part of the cemetery," he said. "It's out of sight from up here. The man who mows the grass has been instructed not to disturb any flowers. Has the marker been damaged?"

"Well, there is—"

"No, sir," Kendra cut me off before I could say anything about the hand carved on the back. "We just thought it was mysterious that somebody would suddenly start putting flowers on that old grave."

"Especially in the middle of the night," I added, just to make it seem creepier. As little as I like mysteries, if it looked like there was one, maybe Kendra and I wouldn't look so dumb in front of the adults.

"I agree, it's odd," the pastor said, "but no harm has been done, so I wouldn't be too concerned about it. I will tell the caretaker to keep his eyes open."

He shook everyone's hand one more time and turned back into the church.

"That didn't exactly solve the mystery, Mom," Kendra said.

Before her mother could say anything, my Gramma spoke sharply. "Why do you have to go meddling in something that's none of your business? Why can't you leave well enough alone?"

The other adults looked at her funny. Gramma Patterson never raises her voice to me, her only grandson.

"You mark my words," she said, shaking her finger at us like an old crone in a fairy tale, "if you start poking around down there, you may find out more than you want to know. More than any of us want to know."

Kendra and I exchanged a long glance. If an adult was telling us to stay out of something, what better reason did we need to get into it?

꧁ ❦ ꧂

Chapter 3

FINALLY, THE LAST week of school. Just like Kendra predicted, fresh flowers appeared on Amanda's grave on Monday, Wednesday, and Friday. By Friday afternoon Kendra was bouncing around like it was Christmas Eve.

"Now we've got nothing to do but work on this case," she said as we rode the bus home. "We can take all summer if we have to."

"Yeah, great," I said. I wasn't really listening to her. I was already dreading that last walk up the aisle to the door of the bus. Getting past Dwayne the last day of school was like getting past a monster in a video game. He'd tripped me when I got on the bus. Now, the way he was turned around in his seat, grinning at me, I figured he was determined to get in enough kicks and shoves to last for the summer.

"But if my plan works," Kendra said, "we'll have the case solved before breakfast on Monday."

Before breakfast? She seemed to be talking about something awfully early. Maybe I'd better listen. "What plan?" I asked, but then the bus stopped.

I let Kendra walk in front of me, like my mom taught me to do. Just as she got to where Dwayne was sitting, she turned around and said, "Hey, Steve ..." When she turned, her backpack, loaded with everything out of her desk, caught Dwayne right in the face. He sprawled back in his seat. His arms and legs flopped like a puppet that's been cut loose from its strings.

"Sorry!" Kendra called as we ran down the steps. The sound of the door closing behind us meant I had escaped.

"Thanks," I said. We both looked up at Dwayne's angry face pressed against the window of the bus as it pulled away.

"Thanks for what? Accidents happen. Boy, this backpack sure is heavy." She smiled as she shifted it up on her shoulder.

"Now, do you want to hear about my plan to learn who the Flower Freak is?"

"Do I have any choice?"

She stuck her tongue out at me. "The only way we're going to find out who the Flower Freak is, is to be there when he—or she—does it. And since he—or she—does it early in the morning, we've got to get there even earlier."

"You mean we'll come down in the middle of the night?"

"No, just real early in the morning."

"Do you really think our parents will say, 'Sure, go ahead. Prowl around in a graveyard. Try to get a look at somebody who could be a maniac'? My mom would freak out if I asked her."

Kendra looked at me like my math teacher does when she's explaining how to multiply fractions and I just don't get it. "Nobody's going to hurt us because they won't know we're there. We'll hide behind the bushes on that side of the cemetery. Our parents won't even know we're gone. We'll set our clocks for five-thirty. We can be back home before they get up."

I groaned. "Five-thirty! On the first Monday of summer vacation?"

⊰ C3 ❧ ⊱

When the alarm went off on Monday morning I dragged myself out of bed. I had put the clock on the floor beside my bed the night before so the alarm wouldn't have to buzz for long. Usually I have to put it across the room or I just turn it off, roll over, and go back to sleep. It's hard to wake me up in the morning. Mom says I get that from my dad.

Slipping on my jeans and a t-shirt, I waited a minute to be sure Mom hadn't heard the alarm. I left a note explaining where I was going lying on my bed in plain view. I didn't want Mom to panic if she found my bed empty. Then I started down the hall.

I had just gotten past the door to my mom's room when I heard an awful noise, kind of a roaring and buzzing combined. *Skzzkzz!* I froze. There it was again. *Skzzkzz!* It was coming from Mom's room.

Her door was open just enough for me to see in with one eye. She was asleep and everything was quiet. Then, suddenly, *Skzzkzz!* She was snoring, as loud as I had ever heard my grandparents snore. At least I could tell I hadn't waked her up.

As I opened the front door, I noticed my baseball bat propped beside it. I picked it up and slipped out.

Kendra was waiting for me behind her garage. It was barely light enough for me to see her family's picnic blanket draped over her shoulder.

"Why did you bring your bat?" she whispered. "Do you think the Flower Freak is going to shag flies for you?"

"I just picked it up on my way out. We might need it. You never know. Which way are we going?" I asked before she could say anything else about my bat. I did feel kind of stupid carrying it, but a little safer, too. "Through the field is shorter."

A large, unplowed field starts behind Kendra's backyard and runs downhill behind the church and along the cemetery. That field and the rest of our subdivision used to be part of a farm. All that's left of the farm now is an old barn that tilts to one side like even a light breeze could blow it over.

Kendra squinched up her nose in disgust. "There's all kinds of snakes and bugs in those weeds. And I'm wearing shorts. The briars would tear up my legs."

"You should've worn jeans, like me."

"It's too hot for jeans. Let's go down the road. Nobody's going to see us this early in the morning."

The sky was turning pink as we walked along our street, Lakeview Drive. The name isn't exactly true. The only view of the lake is from the top of a couple of houses at the end of the street, across from the church. And then only when there aren't any leaves on the trees.

We entered the cemetery, like we always did, on the row where Moniqa was buried. I stood back while Kendra stopped beside her grave and put her hand on the stone. Then, following Kendra's plan, we hid in the hedge between the field and the cemetery, as close to the grave as we dared to get.

"What do we do if somebody does show up?" I said.

"We'll see what direction they came from, what kind of car they're driving, and then go home in time for breakfast."

Kendra's blanket cushioned us some as we stretched out on our stomachs on the hard, dry ground. Her head was pointed northeast and mine northwest, so we could watch for somebody coming from either direction.

The color of Amanda's tombstone changed from gray to pink as the sun hit it. Kendra whispered, "I wonder how she died."

"Probably from getting up too early in the morning." I couldn't stop myself from yawning.

"I dreamed about her last night," Kendra said.

"Amanda? How can you dream about her? You don't know anything about her."

"Well, it started out as a dream about Moniqa."

Kendra told me she dreamed about her sister a lot.

"We were playing, but not in our yard. We were down here by this tree. And she was wearing a long, old-fashioned dress and a sun-bonnet, like in *Little House on the Prairie*. Then, somehow it wasn't Moniqa any more. I couldn't see her face because of the sun-bonnet, but I knew it was Amanda."

"What were you playing?"

"Hide-and-seek. She hid behind that tree. She was giggling because I couldn't catch her. Then it was like her tombstone popped up out of nowhere, and she hid behind it. I could hear her laughing, but I couldn't find her."

"Weird," I said. What else could I say?

We were quiet for a few minutes. Then I worried out loud, "What if the Flower Freak sees us?" I gripped my bat.

"As dark as it is in these bushes, he'll see your white face before he sees me," Kendra said.

"How long are we going to wait?" I yawned again.

"As long as it takes."

Neither of us said anything else and, since we weren't watching each other, neither of us knew when the other one went to sleep.

❦ C380 ❧

Somebody was shaking my arm and whispering my name. "Steve! Wake up! He's here!"

"Just ten more minutes," I mumbled. A hand clamped over my mouth.

"Hush!" Kendra whispered in my ear.

I jerked away from her hand. "What are you doing here? Where am I?" As my eyes came into focus I recognized the hedge and started to remember. Then I saw the man. "Who's he?"

Kendra tried to shush me, but it was too late

The man turned his head. He stood up, looking in our direction. He had heard us!

"Steve, run!" Kendra leaped up from the blanket and took off across the field. Forget thorns and snakes.

As I jumped to my feet I heard the man call, "Hey! Wait!"

Kendra was running across the field straight toward her house. I ran along the hedge. We had gone about twenty yards when Kendra suddenly yelled and fell. I expected her to bounce right back up, but she stayed down and I could hear her moaning. I looked back toward Amanda's grave, as scared as I've ever been.

The man was still standing there, just shaking his head and smiling. He hadn't even been chasing us! But when he saw Kendra wasn't getting back up, he pushed his way through the hedge, picked up my bat, and started toward the spot where she had fallen.

One part of my brain was telling me to run to Kendra's house and get help. Nobody would hear me calling from this far away. But what if the man tried to hurt Kendra? He could get to her and be gone before I could get anybody back down the hill. I looked around quickly, hoping to find something—a big stick, a rock. But there was nothing I could use.

I was afraid to get too close to the man, but I had to protect Kendra, so I moved toward her. I wasn't sure what I could do. I just knew I had to do something.

CHAPTER 4

I GOT TO KENDRA first and grabbed her arm. "Come on! Get up!"

"I can't. I think my ankle's broken. It hurts so bad."

I looked up at the man, who was approaching us slowly. I hoped I looked brave. I hadn't been this afraid since I tried to stop Dwayne from pushing another kid off a swing at recess last fall. I got nothing to show for that but a bad scrape on my chin and a torn shirt, and the other boy still got pushed off the swing.

Kendra was lying on her side, clutching her left ankle and crying. The long dry grass whispered as the man pushed it aside and came closer to us. I kept my hand on her shoulder, as if I could snatch her away from him.

He stopped a couple of feet away from us. "I guess this is yours." He flipped my bat over so the handle was pointed toward me. I reached up and took it from him.

"Don't choke up if you decide to take a swing at me." He knelt beside Kendra. "What happened, hon?" His voice was kind, like a teacher or a doctor.

"I stepped in a hole," Kendra said through her gritted teeth. "It hurts like ... blazes." Tears streaked her dirty cheeks.

"Don't try to move yet," the man said sympathetically. "Let me check it." He unclenched her hands and gently felt her foot and around her ankle. "I don't feel any broken bones. Let's see if you can stand on it at all."

He took her arm and slowly helped her up. "Grab a hand, son," he told me.

Kendra managed to get to her feet but could not put enough weight on her left foot to walk.

"We'd better get you home," the man said. "Where do you kids live?"

I pointed. "At the top of the hill."

The man rolled his eyes and groaned a bit. "That figures. It's about as far to my car as it is to your house, and I'm going to have to carry this young lady either way." He sighed. "We might as well get going."

He put one arm around Kendra's waist. "Put your arms around my neck and get ready to jump." He braced himself. "Okay. *Up you go!*" Kendra jumped as high as she could with only one leg to push with, and he caught under her knees with his other arm.

"Comfy?" he asked with a smile.

"Yeah," Kendra replied. "I mean, yes, sir." Our parents try to teach us manners and sometimes we remember them.

"Good. Now, young man—Steve, I believe I heard your friend call you—if you would pick up the blanket, we'll make our way up this slope that is starting to look like Mount Everest. We may have to establish a base camp somewhere along the way."

I didn't understand all the mountain-climbing talk, but I didn't feel afraid of the man. I ran to the hedge and picked up the blanket. The man worked his way through the weeds back to the cemetery.

"The footing's better here," he said. "I don't want to step in another hole, carrying you."

Kendra looked up the hill. "It's a long way."

"I would suggest that you walk, but we don't know how badly your ankle is hurt. Did it pop when you fell?"

Kendra nodded her head.

"That sounds like what happened to me several years ago in a softball game," the man said.

"You play softball?" I asked.

"Well, I *played* softball until I tore up my ankle sliding into second. As soon as I hit the base, everybody on the field heard the pop. But I got up, said I was all right, and played the rest of the game. I was the pitcher, and we just had nine guys to play, so if I had gone out of the game, we wouldn't have been able to continue. I stayed in for four more innings."

"Boy, you were brave!" I said.

"No, I was dumb. I ended up on crutches for two weeks. It was a month before I could walk without limping. The doctor said, if I had sat down right after I hurt it, it wouldn't have been nearly as bad. We'll get some ice on this and hopefully you won't have too much trouble with it."

"But I have my tennis lesson tomorrow," Kendra said.

The man shook his head. "You'll need to be off this for a few days. I'll bet the doctor says you need RICE."

"Rice? How would eating rice help a sprained ankle?"

"RICE stands for Rest, Ice, Compression, and Elevation. That's what the ER doctor told me. You'll have to wrap this tightly and keep your foot propped up as much as you can for a few days."

I studied him as we worked our way up the hill. He was wearing a plain cotton shirt and a pair of jeans. His hair was light brown with some gray in it. He looked a little older than Kendra's father, but not as old as my Grampa Patterson.

"Whew! I'm going to have to rest for a minute, kids." He placed Kendra gently on the ground and we sat down. The graves around us were from the 1930s and 1940s.

"We haven't actually introduced ourselves," he said. We told him our names. "My name is David Crisp," he said. "Most people call me Doc, because my middle initial is 'O'."

"What's that stand for?" I asked.

"If I tell you, will you tell me why you're out here at this unhallowed hour?"

"It must be awful," Kendra said. She glanced at me, and I nodded. "Deal," she said. "You go first."

"You're a pretty assertive young woman, aren't you?" Doc said with a slight smile.

"If that means bossy, you're right," I said.

Doc laughed. There was something about him that made me feel safe. All my mother's warnings about not talking to strangers were running through my head, but this stranger hadn't done anything to scare me so far. I was glad he hadn't suggested getting in his car, though. I wouldn't have done that or let him take Kendra. And I still had a tight grip on my bat.

"Well," he said, "the 'O' stands for 'Oscar'. Now, do I look like an Oscar? Wait, don't answer that. Just tell me what you were doing out here."

"We wanted to know who the Flower Freak was," I said.

"Steve!" Kendra squealed.

"The Flower Freak?" Doc said, but he looked like he thought it was funny.

"Yes, sir. We saw the flowers on that grave, and we wondered who was putting them there. We started calling him the Flower Freak, just as a joke."

"It's shorter than 'the person who's putting flowers on the grave'," Kendra said. "We didn't mean anything by it."

"I've been called worse," Doc said. "And now you know who the Flower Freak is."

"But who *are* you?" Kendra persisted. "And why did you put flowers on that little girl's grave? Are you a relative of hers?"

Doc smiled and flexed his arms like they were sore. "Well, you kids have gone to a lot of trouble. I guess you deserve an explanation. You're going to be disappointed, though. It's not really anything mysterious."

He leaned back and took a deep breath. "I teach history at Halley College. It's a small school in Indiana. I'm staying in one of those cottages across the road. The one with the blue door. I've been putting the flowers on Amanda's grave because she seems lonely, like me."

From the look Kendra gave me, I thought she was embarrassed, like I was. It hadn't occurred to us that we might be spying on something personal.

"You see," Doc went on, "my wife and I had been spending our vacations at this lake for years. We own a house on the other side of it. But she died of cancer in January." He looked up over our heads and cleared his throat. "I came down here after my school closed for the summer, like we always did, but I couldn't stand being in our house without her. So I rented a cottage and put the house up for sale. I'm just staying around until I can find a buyer. And because I don't like being alone in our house in Indiana either."

Kendra shifted her leg and rubbed her ankle. "I'm really sorry about your wife. How did you find out about Amanda?"

"I walked up here one day, looking at the names and dates on the markers. I can't stop being a historian. Then I noticed that one grave, off by itself. When I saw it was a little girl, it made me sad. My wife and I never had any children, and I felt Amanda and I both were very alone. So I started bringing her flowers and sitting there for a few minutes. You may be too young to understand why I wanted to do that."

"Why'd you come out here so early in the morning?" I said. "You can come any time. Who would care?"

Doc smiled. "I've taught eight o'clock classes on Mondays, Wednesdays and Fridays for years, and I can't stop getting up early, even in the summer. I like that time of day. Things are quiet and private then. Except when some nosy kids spy on me."

We could tell from his expression that he was teasing, and we smiled back at him.

"Why do you think Amanda's buried out there all by herself?" Kendra asked.

"I don't know," Doc said. "I'm sure her parents must be around here somewhere. Speaking of parents, I'm surprised yours would let you out this early in the morning to go stalking some stranger."

"Uh ... they didn't exactly 'let' us," Kendra admitted.

Doc straightened up. "You mean your parents don't know where you are?" This time he did sound kind of mad.

"No, sir," we both said softly.

"They're going to be worried sick." Doc got up and brushed off his pants. "Come on! Everybody up! We've got to get you home immediately."

The light was on in the Jordans' kitchen when Doc carried Kendra into her backyard. I trailed along with the blanket draped over my shoulder and my bat resting on it.

"See, they're up," Doc said. "I'll bet they've already called the police."

"I'll bet they don't even know I'm gone," Kendra said. "The door to my room was closed."

When Mrs. Jordan answered the door we could tell from her reaction that Kendra was right. Her mother's mouth dropped open and her hands flew up, like somebody in a movie. It would have been funny if I hadn't been so scared.

"Kendra Louise!" she cried. "What on earth ... ?"

"Hi, Mom. I sprained my ankle," Kendra said sheepishly. "It's not too bad. This is Doc ... Mr. Crisp. He carried me home."

"Oh, thank you!" Mrs. Jordan said. Her hands fluttered over Kendra. "Where are you hurt? What happened? Let me see, Baby."

"Where do you want me to put her down?" Doc asked. He was puffing louder and getting redder by the minute.

"Oh, let's see. Here—" Mrs. Jordan pulled a chair out from the kitchen table. Kendra's cat, lying in ambush for any bacon left unguarded on the table, meowed and jumped down.

"Tom? Tom! Come here—please!" Mrs. Jordan called to her husband.

With Kendra and me trying to talk over one another, it took a few minutes to explain everything. By then Kendra had an ice pack on her ankle and Doc had been introduced to her parents.

When she finally felt she had the situation under control, Kendra's mother called my mother. "Robin, you're not going to believe what *your* son and *my* daughter have been up to."

Kendra and I looked at one another nervously. When our mothers started talking about us that way, we were in trouble.

Mrs. Jordan listened on the phone while my mom said something, then she said. "You'd better get over here right away ... No, Steve's standing in my kitchen right now. He looks like he'd trade all his baseball cards for some place to hide. ... All right, the back door's open. We'll see you in a minute."

While we waited, Kendra's father offered Doc a cup of coffee. As he poured, he asked, "You say you're at Halley College?"

"Yes. In the History Department." Doc added a spoonful of sugar and a little cream to his coffee.

"There's a guy in the accounting department where I work who used to be in the business office at Halley, I believe."

"That must be Ken DePree," Doc said.

"Yes, that's him," Kendra's dad said. "So you know him?"

"My wife and I played bridge in a group with Ken and his wife. We let them use our home on the lake—it's over on the other side—for a vacation. They liked the place so much Ken found a job in the area. We used to get together and play bridge with them during the summers after they moved down here."

I slipped Kendra a thumbs-up sign. I could see her dad looked at Doc differently now. He knew somebody who knew Doc. It made me feel better about him, too. He wasn't a total stranger, somebody we might have to be afraid of.

The back door pushed open and my mom stuck her head in.

She's thirty-four, with short brown hair and blue eyes. She hadn't put on her make-up yet or done more than run a brush through her hair. I like her best that way. Once she's ready to go to work, she looks like she doesn't quite belong to me somehow.

"Is it safe to come in?" she asked with a nervous laugh. "The disaster over yet?"

"It's not as bad as all that," Kendra's dad assured her. "The kids gave us a little surprise, but they've done worse. We may have to shoot Kendra Louise, though."

Kendra rolled her eyes. She knew another of his awful jokes was coming.

"That's what they do to horses when they tear up a leg and they're no good for anything any more." Her dad sounded completely serious.

"Daddy! It's just a sprain."

"Yeah, but you'll miss a couple of tennis lessons, lose your next tournament. That means you'll be behind schedule to get into Wimbledon. Before you know it, you'll be over the hill, useless. Then we'll have to shoot you." He leaned over and hugged her.

My mother ignored Mr. Jordan's lame joke and looked at Kendra's ankle closely. "How're you feeling, hon?"

"The ice is helping."

"Good. I hope it's not serious." Then she turned to me. "As for you, young man ..." From the tone in her voice I was sure she was going to ground me for the rest of the summer.

"It was my idea," Kendra said quickly.

"But he went along with it," Mom said, still looking at me. "Didn't you think I'd be worried?"

"I left you a note," I said weakly. "I thought we'd be back before you got up."

Doc cleared his throat. "I don't mean to interfere in a family matter, but I am the reason these youngsters were out this morning. I was putting flowers on that old grave, and Steve and Kendra were just naturally curious. I think they've learned something from the experience and won't do anything like this again. Will you, kids?"

"No, sir!" we both said.

"And who are you, if I may ask? What grave are you talking

about?" The way Mom snapped at Doc, I could tell she hadn't had her coffee yet.

By the time the whole situation had been explained again, everyone had time to cool down and notice they were hungry. Kendra picked up a slice of bacon off the plate on the table and broke off a piece for the cat, who was rubbing against her leg and meowing.

"Why don't we have some breakfast," her mother suggested, "before Kendra feeds all the bacon to the cat. Professor Crisp, won't you stay and eat with us?"

"Please stay," Kendra and I said together. We wanted him to. Besides, we knew we wouldn't get fussed at in front of company.

"Thanks, but I'm going back down to the cemetery. Steve and Kendra have gotten me to thinking about something that hadn't occurred to me before. There are a few puzzles about that old grave I'd like to clear up."

CHAPTER 5

"Do you understand what I'm saying?" my mom asked as she picked up her keys and purse. "*Do you understand?*"

"Yes, ma'am," I said as I got out the milk for my cereal.

"Well, I hope you do. We were going to try this new arrangement because I thought I could trust you to spend some time alone this summer while I'm at work. But after that stunt yesterday, I don't know if it's going to work."

"It was Kendra's idea, Mom. We won't do anything like that again. I promise."

"You'd better not. If I can't trust you to stay here, you'll have to spend the day in the store where I can keep an eye on you."

"Come on, Mom! I'm not a baby."

"You're going to have to prove that to me, Steve. I'll call you at lunch."

I let out a long breath when she closed the door. Like she did every summer, my mom had arranged for me to stay with the Jordans while she worked. This year I didn't actually have to spend the whole day at Kendra's house, but I was supposed to check with Mrs. Jordan once in a while and get her permission before I went anywhere. I would eat lunch with them, too. We had had a *long* talk last night about how much Mom was worried about us sneaking out to go to the cemetery.

The rain that started yesterday afternoon was still coming down as I ate breakfast. I moved from where I usually sit at the table. I don't like looking out our back window when I'm home by myself and the weather's all cloudy and gloomy. It makes old Mrs. Bradford's house at the top of the hill look creepy, like the house in a scary movie that nobody's supposed to go into.

After breakfast I got out my baseball cards and sorted and resorted them. Sometimes I like to group them by teams.

Sometimes I put my favorites into an All-Star team. Since I play second base, today I was pulling out all the second basemen and comparing them.

The rain stopped about ten-thirty. I got permission from Mrs. Jordan to ride my bike down to Philips' store to buy some new cards. The trip back up the hill is kind of a pain, but it's fun to go flying down it on a bike. When it snowed a couple of years ago, my mom brought home a sled from her hardware store. That was *really* fun.

The sign in front says Philips' is a 'Grocery Store,' but the only food they sell is stuff tourists and kids like: snack food, microwave dinners, and some canned goods. Most of the shelves hold fishing gear, sunglasses, souvenir t-shirts, and mugs with 'Kentucky' on the side and 'Made in China' on the bottom. The place smells like bait, especially when it gets warm in the summer.

"Well, if it isn't my old neighbor," Mr. Philips said from behind the counter as I walked in. He's a tall guy, about my mom's age, with dark thin hair, a long face divided in half by a mustache, and a stomach that hangs over his belt. He lives over the store. He paid a lot of attention to Mom and me when we owned the tourist cottages next door and lived in one of them. After Dad left, Mr. Philips used to drop over to 'see if you need anything.' I don't think Mom likes him. If we need a gallon of milk or bread, she drives an extra mile to the next store rather than run down to Philips'.

I picked out two packs of baseball cards and got out my money.

"Here, have another one." Mr. Philips tossed a pack of cards into the bag with the first two. Mom tells me never to take anything from him, but how could a free pack of baseball cards hurt?

"Say hello to your mom for me!" he called from the door as I pushed my bike across the gravel parking lot to the road. "Tell her to let me know if there's anything I can do for her!"

"I will," I promised over my shoulder, even though my mom has told me she never wants to hear his name mentioned.

I was halfway across the parking lot when a pick-up truck pulled in, cutting in front of me and making me jump out of the way. The truck growled to a halt in front of the store and the driver gunned the engine before he shut it off. Dwayne Mitchell was leaning out the window on the passenger side. His father,

smoking a cigarette and wearing a white t-shirt and jeans, went
into the store with a bait pail. I had never seen Mr. Mitchell
before, but I would have recognized him even if Dwayne hadn't
been with him. He wore the same smirk, with the right side of
his mouth twisted up, that made Dwayne's face so ugly.

Dwayne got out and strutted over to where I was standing.
My first instinct was to push my bike hard and try to get to the
road before he got to me. But I knew he would just chase me, and
I would have to pedal uphill. I might as well stand still and endure
it. Surely his father wouldn't take too long getting the bait.

"Hi, ho, Steverino!" Dwayne said. He picked that up from
reruns of some old TV show. His family has a satellite dish and
a big-screen TV. Dwayne likes to remind other kids of that. We
wonder how it all fits in their trailer, but nobody dares to ask.

"Hello, Dwayne. Are you going fishing?" Maybe if I could
get him talking ...

"Yeah, my *dad*'s takin' me. Too bad you don't have a *dad*
to take you." As he got closer to me, he began to scuff his feet,
kicking up gravel onto my bike.

"Watch it! You're going to scratch the paint."

"Who're you tellin' to watch it, shrimp?" Dwayne grabbed
the front of my shirt. He loomed over me, almost a head taller.

His father came out of the store. "Hey, Dwayne, throw that
one back! He's too little."

Dwayne shoved me and sent me staggering into my bike.
As I tried to untangle myself he and his father both laughed like
it was the funniest thing they'd ever seen.

"Put this bait in the back of the truck," his father said.

When Dwayne took the pail it almost slipped from his hand.
Some of the smelly water in it splashed onto his father's jeans.

"You clumsy little ... !" his father yelled.

Dwayne must have known a blow was coming. He managed
to scrunch up his shoulder to block some of it, but it still caught
him on the ear and turned him halfway around. His father let out
a string of cuss words. The only time I had heard language like
that before was from Dwayne on the playground at recess.

Dwayne wouldn't look at me as he climbed into the back of
the truck. I watched them roar out of sight, with the radio blaring
over the glass-pack muffler.

Maybe I don't have a dad, I thought, but at least I don't have Dwayne's dad.

The sun came out as I pedaled back up the hill. Doc was walking around in the cemetery. He waved at me and started walking toward the road, carrying something in one hand, so I stopped.

"Good morning, Steve," he said. "I'm glad I ran into you. I came by your house a few minutes ago, but there was nobody home. I wanted to give you this."

He held out a wrapped package. From the size and weight I could tell it was a book, a big one. "Thanks," I said, even though big books aren't my favorite kind of gift. I like to read, but when somebody gives you a book it's usually not one you'd pick out yourself.

"I dropped off something for Kendra, too. Her mother said she was asleep. The pain pills they gave her at the emergency room knocked her out."

"What are you looking for in the cemetery?" I asked.

"You and Kendra have made me more curious about why Amanda's grave is off by itself. I've never seen anything like that in a cemetery before."

"If you figure out why, don't tell Kendra. She wants to solve this 'case' by herself. I hope she does soon, so we can do something that's more fun."

⋘ ⟡ ⋙

When I got home I opened Doc's present. It was a book about the history of baseball! At first I just looked at the pictures. There were even some from as long ago as Amanda's time. The players wore suspenders and had big mustaches. If they had gloves at all, they were flat and shapeless, like the one my grandfather showed me that belonged to *his* grandfather. There weren't any stands around the fields in those days. People stood or sat almost on top of the players.

When the phone rang I was surprised to see how long I had been reading. I thought my mom was calling to check on me, but it was Kendra.

"Are you coming over this morning?" she asked, but it sounded more like, 'Why haven't you come over this morning?'

"I didn't want to bother you. I thought you were sleeping."

"I'm up now. Why don't you come over? We can talk or do something."

I crossed the street and let myself in Kendra's house. They gave me a key, because they consider me one of their family.

Kendra was sitting on the sofa with an open book and her cat in her lap. His name is Clyde. Her swollen left foot, wrapped in an elastic bandage, was propped on a pillow with a heating pad under it. X-rays hadn't shown any broken bones, but for at least several days she would need the crutches lying on the floor beside her.

"Guess who I saw a little while ago," I said.

"How would I know?" Kendra snapped. "My foot hurts." She's usually an easy person to get along with, but, if she's sick and has to sit or lie still for long, she starts feeling sorry for herself and gets really crabby.

"You want to be a detective," I said. "Why don't you figure it out?" I had meant to tell her my news, but not if she was going to bite my head off. Hiding in the bushes was *her* idea, after all.

Kendra winced in pain as she sat up straighter. Clyde got up and moved to the other end of the sofa. "I can't figure out anything without evidence," she said. "You haven't given me the first clue."

"I was working on my baseball cards," I began.

She cut right in. "So you went to Philips' store to get some more. You went past the cemetery, of course. And the only person you could have seen who would have been worth mentioning to me would be Doc. Right?"

"Yeah. How did you guess?"

"I didn't *guess*. You gave me a clue. What was he doing?"

"He was reading some of the other grave markers."

"Did you talk to him?"

"For a couple of minutes. He gave me a book."

"He brought me a book *and* a box of candy, but I was asleep when he came by. He's a neat guy."

I wasn't ticked off that she had gotten the candy. She deserved special treatment because of her sprained ankle. I had to agree about Doc. Any man who played ball hard enough to hurt himself and still stay in the game rated pretty high in my opinion. "What kind of book is yours?"

Kendra held up the book she'd been reading. "It's some stories about a detective named Sherlock Holmes. Doc's note says he's always liked them and he hopes I will."

"Oh, brother." Now I felt betrayed. How could a man who liked baseball also like detective stories?

Kendra ignored me. "Help me get to the computer. I want to show you something."

I handed her the crutches and made sure no furniture was in her way as she hobbled to the Jordans' computer workspace in a small room off their kitchen. I couldn't keep Clyde from running around her crutches and trying to rub up against them. Kendra moved the mouse and the screen came to life.

"This is Halley College's web site," she said, "where Doc teaches." *Click.* "Here's the History Department's home page." *Click.* "And there's a picture of the professors."

Doc stood on the left of a group of five people. "Cool. He seems like a nice guy."

"Yeah," Kendra said. "Maybe we could go down to the cemetery and see him."

"I bet he's gone by now. It'll take you the rest of the day to get there on your crutches." On the tennis court Kendra is graceful as a dancer, but on crutches she was like a new-born colt trying to get its legs under control. "Could your mom drive us down?"

"She went to get groceries. She won't be back until lunch. You could ride me down on your bike."

"Don't you think we'd better ask?"

"You're such a wuss, Steve."

"Hey, we're lucky we didn't get grounded yesterday. I think we'd better be really careful for a few days."

"Okay, I'll call her cell phone."

I brought Kendra the phone from her kitchen and she dialed her mom's cell number. We both jumped when a phone rang in the utility room.

"She forgot it," Kendra said. "Well, I tried. Let's go. I don't want to wait. Doc'll be gone before she gets back. Help me up."

⤙ ₢₿ ⤚

CHAPTER 6

A FEW MINUTES later we were on our way down the hill to the cemetery on my bike. I stood on the pedals. Kendra sat on the seat and balanced her crutches across her lap. With her other hand she held on to my belt. Every time the bike wobbled she shrieked and giggled. Doc was walking toward the road to see what was going on long before I brought the bike to a stop.

Doc smiled and shook his head. "I don't believe you two!" He stepped across the ditch to help Kendra off the bike.

"I wanted to thank you for the candy and the book. Sherlock Holmes is really a smart detective. I wish I was that smart."

"It's not just a matter of being smart," Doc said. "Some people train themselves to observe closely and to remember what they see, hear, or read. And they ask questions."

Kendra balanced on one foot and put the crutches under her arms. "I've got one big question," she said. "How am I going to get across this ditch?"

"Why don't you pole vault over it?" I suggested.

"Hah, hah," Kendra looked up at Doc apologetically. "I need your help again, I guess." Doc handed her crutches up to me and then picked Kendra up, like he did the day before, and lifted her over the ditch. Once in the cemetery she could get around on her crutches, although the ground was spongy in spots from the heavy rain.

"What are you doing?" I asked as we walked slowly across the cemetery. "Looking for another lonely little girl?"

"Actually I am," Doc said. "Your question about why Amanda is buried by herself got me to thinking: What about her family? Did she have any brothers or sisters? Could they be buried somewhere else in here? If not, why is she the only person in the cemetery buried off by herself?"

"That's kind of a ... mystery, isn't it?" Kendra said.

I sighed. "I *knew* you were going to say that."

Doc laughed. "'Mystery' might be too strong a word. It's just a question I can't answer yet."

"Yeah." I was glad to have our new friend on my side now. "It all happened more than a hundred years ago. You can't solve a mystery that old."

"I didn't say that," Doc pointed out. "Historians do it all the time. In fact, historians in some ways are detectives whose 'cases' just happen to be hundreds or thousands of years old."

"I thought historians looked stuff up in books," I said.

"Somebody has to write the books first," Doc said. "Think of it this way: What do detectives try to do?"

"They try to fit clues together and figure out what happened in a case," Kendra said quickly. She's always the first one to raise her hand in class to answer a question.

"That's exactly what historians try to do," Doc said. "And historians and detectives have to look at things carefully from all angles. Sometimes they consult experts in other fields— pathology, firearms, and so on."

"Yeah, Sherlock Holmes knows about inks, paper, mud, perfumes, all kinds of stuff," Kendra said. "Where they come from, how they're made, everything. How does he keep all that in his head?"

"Well, he is a fictional character, but the man who wrote about him, Arthur Conan Doyle, had to know all that stuff. As you read more of the stories you'll see Holmes is presented as someone who has read everything he can get his hands on, and he remembers everything he reads."

"Why doesn't he just look it up on the internet?" I said.

Kendra rolled her eyes at me. "The stories were written a long time ago, before there were any computers."

"Sherlock Holmes' brain was as full of information as a computer," Doc said. "He could make connections between things that other people didn't notice. That's how real detectives and historians try to work, even if they can't be as brilliant as Holmes. Sometimes they find an important clue by accident. Sometimes they overlook obvious things until someone else points them out."

"I don't feel like a historian or a detective. I just want

to know what happened to Amanda's family." I said that for Kendra's benefit. What I really wanted was to get the whole business finished so I could get back to my new baseball cards. Who knew how many rookies or superstars were hidden in those unopened packs?

"Maybe nothing happened to them," Doc said. "All we know is that they aren't buried with her, and that's odd."

I could see the wheels turning in Kendra's head. She wouldn't quit until she had the answers she wanted. And she wouldn't let me quit.

"Why don't we go through the cemetery and see if they're buried in some other part?" Kendra suggested. She had sat as long as she could stand it.

"Do we have to do the whole cemetery?" I protested. "The old part's down here. Isn't that where they're likely to be?"

Doc nodded. "Steve's right. Her parents probably didn't live past 1900. We need to look in the section of really old graves."

For an hour we read tombstones. Kendra found it easier to hop from stone to stone than to use her crutches. But we didn't find even one Allen. Then Doc bought us drinks at Philips' store and we sat under the tree by Amanda's grave

"So, what have we learned?" Doc asked.

"There were people buried here before Amanda was," I said. "The date on her grave isn't the earliest."

"So they deliberately put her off in the corner, didn't they?" Kendra said.

Doc nodded and took a sip of his drink. "I think so."

"Like they didn't want her around the others," Kendra went on. "Do you think she might have been black?"

"I doubt it," Doc said. "Remember, in 1862 President Lincoln hadn't issued the Emancipation Proclamation yet, so African-Americans were still slaves."

"But the Emancipation Proclamation only applied to the states that seceded," Kendra said. "Kentucky didn't secede."

Doc raised his eyebrows like he was impressed. "That's right. Not many people realize that."

"We covered it in social studies this year," I said. But I had forgotten it.

Doc picked up a stick and scratched on the ground. "I don't

think a slave child would be buried in this cemetery. And people are buried here in family groups. There's not another child in this cemetery without at least one parent buried close to them."

"There sure are a lot of young children buried here," I said. It made me feel creepy to notice how many there actually were.

"Yeah," Kendra said. "I wonder what happened to them."

"Life was rough for people in those days," Doc said, "whether they were slave or free, black or white. They worked hard and didn't have the things that make our lives easy. There weren't many doctors or hospitals. Most of our medicines were unknown then. Even what we regard as a simple childhood disease, like measles, was a dreaded plague to them. Some diseases that were common at the time of the Civil War—like smallpox—have been eliminated now. There are at least a dozen tombstones in this cemetery from October of 1862. There may have been an outbreak of some disease around here then."

"But we can't know what Amanda died of, can we?" Kendra asked.

Doc shook his head. "Probably not. Historians can study old bones and tell something about the person they belonged to. Some diseases leave traces in the bones. But, even if we could get permission to exhume the body, I'd be surprised if we could learn much from it."

"Did you find any other stones with anything carved on the back of them?" I asked.

Doc looked at me in surprise. "I haven't noticed anything like that. Why do you ask?"

"There's something on the back of Amanda's stone," Kendra said. "Steve saw it the other day. Come on, we'll show you."

Doc followed us to the back of Amanda's tombstone and knelt down and examined the faint carving. "It does appear to be pointing toward the road, but I can't imagine why anybody would have carved it. I'll have to think about it."

"I think better on a full stomach," I said.

"Good point," Doc said. "It is close to lunchtime. You'd better be getting home."

"When will we see you again?" Kendra asked. "We've still got a mystery to solve."

"I've got some things to do this afternoon, but I'll be here right on schedule tomorrow morning," Doc said, smiling, "at seven, to put some fresh flowers on Amanda's grave."

"Couldn't you make it more like eight?" I said. "Or maybe after lunch?"

"What difference does it make to you two? You're not going to be here, are you?" Doc smiled at us like he knew a secret. Then Kendra and I started back to the road.

We had covered about half the distance between Amanda's grave and the road when one of Kendra's crutches came down on something hard, but the other one sank into the soft, wet dirt. She was thrown off balance so quickly she couldn't let go of the crutches and get her hands out to brace herself. She hit the ground hard.

Doc and I were hovering over her in a second. "Did you hurt anything?" Doc asked. "Don't move till you're sure."

"I'm okay." Kendra sat up. "What did I hit?"

Scraping aside some dirt, Doc and I uncovered part of what looked like a large flat stone.

"Maybe it's a grave marker that got knocked over," I suggested.

"Maybe it's Amanda's parents!" Kendra struggled to her feet.

"I don't think so," Doc said slowly. "I don't think it's a grave marker at all." He dug down beside it with his fingers. "It's thicker than a tombstone, and it's not finished as smoothly."

Kendra rubbed some dirt from her chin. "What do you suppose it is?"

Doc poked around the edge of the stone. "Without digging up the whole thing I couldn't say, and I wouldn't do that without getting permission from the church. It might be part of the foundation for an old storage building that belonged to the church. I doubt it has anything to do with our little girl, though, so let's just leave it for now."

CHAPTER 7

"COULD WE STOP just a minute?" Kendra asked, as we turned the corner and started to walk down the hill to the church early the next morning. "My arms really hurt. I feel like I've been practicing my serve all day."

"I thought you were in such great shape," I said.

"Crutches use different muscles." She flexed one arm, then the other. "I'd like to see you try and walk on the blasted things for a few hours."

"Yeah, sorry." I started down the hill, walking the way I usually do.

"Slow down," Kendra pleaded. "Downhill is the hardest of all. I get going too fast and I can't stop."

The sun was even with the treetops when we reached the sidewalk leading from the road to the door of the church.

"Let's cut across here," Kendra said. She hobbled almost up to the door, then crossed the lawn and went down through the cemetery. That way she didn't have to climb over the ditch beside the road. And she could stop at her sister's grave for a minute. I had seen her do this more times than I could count. She never said anything, just stood silently with one hand on the tombstone. Since Moniqa was three years younger than us, she didn't play with us much, but I remembered her as a cute little kid.

Kendra sighed, put her crutches back under her arms, and we worked our way down the hill toward Amanda's grave. Kendra was concentrating on placing her crutches on solid ground, so I was the first to notice Doc crossing the road from the cottages.

"Look." I nudged Kendra and pointed. She turned to see that Doc was carrying flowers, but not a handful of wildflowers. This time he had a large bouquet from a flower shop.

"Well, this is an 'unexpected' pleasure," he said as we reached Amanda's grave. "I'm glad you're here. Today is a special day."

"Special? Why?" I asked.

"It's Amanda's birthday." Doc pointed to the grave marker. "You have to pay attention to things you read. And keep the information in your head." He tapped his forehead with one finger.

"June 10th!" Kendra said. "How did I miss that? Sherlock Holmes wouldn't have."

"Is that why you brought the nice flowers?" I asked.

Doc looked hurt. "I thought the others were nice, too, but I decided she ought to have something special for her birthday."

"I'll bet she never had anything like that when she was alive," Kendra said. She and I sat down in front of the tombstone.

"That's true." Doc knelt to remove the old wild flowers and put the new arrangement in their place. "I doubt if she ever had many birthday or Christmas presents. Her parents were probably poor, and the Civil War was going on when she died."

I began singing softly, "Happy birthday to you." Kendra looked at me in surprise, then she and Doc joined in.

When we finished, Kendra said, "I wonder if she was killed in the war."

"I'm no expert on the Civil War," Doc said, "but I do know Kentucky was neutral. In this part of the state the people favored the South. In the east, they favored the North. There wasn't any fighting in this area, as far as I know."

"Is there *any* way we could find out something about Amanda and her family?" Kendra asked. She's the smartest kid I know. Her parents have even more books than my mom, and she's been using a computer since she learned to read. Nothing frustrates her more than not being able to find the answer to a question.

"There might be a story in it for you, Steve," she said.

"Do you like stories?" Doc asked.

"Like them? He writes them." Kendra sounded as proud of me as my mother. "Even had one published in the newspaper."

"I'm impressed," Doc said.

I shrugged. "It was just on the kids' page."

"Well, there are real possibilities for a story here," Doc said.

"But all we know is when she was born and died. We can't just make up the rest of it."

"There might be church records." Doc glanced up the hill at the church. "Lists of members, burial records, that sort of thing."

"Let's go see." Kendra reached for her crutches.

Doc patted her knee. "Relax. There won't be anybody there for a couple of hours yet."

"Could we meet there after breakfast?" Kendra said.

Doc smiled. "I have a better idea. I called your parents last night and told them that if you two made it down here, as I thought you might, I'd like to take you over to the Lodge for breakfast. They said it was fine with them."

We could hardly say 'yes' and 'thank you' fast enough as we scrambled to our feet.

⊰⊱

The Lodge at Lake Barkley is decorated like a big country cabin. It has large wooden beams and pillars and huge windows that give you a view of the lake from every table. It's kind of expensive, so Mom and I don't eat there very often.

"She'll be trying to figure us out all day," Kendra said as the waitress took our order back to the kitchen.

"What do you mean?" Doc said.

"The way she was looking at us, you could tell she didn't understand why a white boy and a black girl are having breakfast with a man who's old enough to be their grandfather."

"How did you two become friends?" Doc asked.

"My parents used to own the cottages you're staying in. When they ... got divorced"—it was still hard for me to say it—"Mom bought the house we live in now. I was five. Kendra's family moved in a couple of months before us. There weren't any other kids our age around, so we started playing together."

The waitress brought Doc a cup of coffee and Kendra and me some orange juice.

"My mom says we were friends before we knew we weren't supposed to," Kendra said. "I remember when we were six, I asked my parents if Steve could spend the night. It freaked them out."

"We don't do that any more," I quickly added.

"Now you just sneak out early in the morning to prowl around in a cemetery," Doc said.

"Uh, yeah," Kendra said. "Stuff like that."

While we waited for our order I looked out over the lake. The surface was calm, with no wind blowing. A few boats bobbed around. I wondered if Dwayne and his dad were in one of them.

Doc followed my gaze. "Do you kids like to fish?"

We both shook our heads.

"You mean you've lived near this lake all your lives, and you don't like fishing?"

"I can't sit still that long," Kendra said.

"We like to ride our bikes or go hiking," I said. "It would be okay with me if the lake was dry, like it used to be. Then there'd be more places to explore."

"I wonder what this area looked like before the lakes," Kendra said.

Doc poured cream into his coffee. "Before white settlers arrived Native Americans lived here. At the time of the American Revolution large herds of buffalo roamed here. The Native Americans used to burn the forests to create more open space for the buffalo because they depended on their hides and meat."

"Then Daniel Boone came through the Cumberland Gap, right?" I said, to show I'd learned something in social studies.

"Right. The Native Americans were pushed west, and white settlers wiped out the buffalo herds to make room for farms."

"What was it like when Amanda lived here?" Kendra asked.

"There were some small towns. Cadiz was here then. But mostly farms that produced a bare living if the people worked hard from sunrise to sunset. Most of these inlets and bays on the lake used to be creeks that ran into the river."

"Did the people here use a lot of slaves?" I asked.

"There were slaves here, in the western part of the state. People in the mountains in eastern Kentuky worked the mines, and didn't use slaves as much. The state was divided about slavery. Soldiers from Kentucky fought on both sides in the Civil War."

"The Presidents on both sides—Abe Lincoln and Jeff Davis—were born in Kentucky," Kendra said. "Our teacher said that shows how the state was split."

"Jefferson Davis was born near here, wasn't he?" Doc said.

Kendra and I nodded. "A few miles east of Hopkinsville," she said. "There's a monument to him there."

"It's a tall thing, with a pointy top." I made an upside-down V with my hands. "Like the Washington Monument."

"An obelisk," Doc said. He took a sip of his coffee.

"Yeah, an obelisk."

"But it's not as tall as the Washington Monument," Kendra said, "and it's made out of concrete, not marble. It's the tallest concrete monument in the country, and the fourth tallest monument of any kind. Three hundred and fifty feet, I think our teacher told us."

"Have you seen it?" Doc asked.

"Our class took a field trip over there last year," I said.

"It looks really tall," Kendra said, "because there's nothing but trees around it."

"And it's kind of scary," I said. "It's got these two windows at the top where you can look out. But they look more like eyes. I felt like Frodo walking up to the Dark Tower."

Doc chuckled. "I'll have to get over there and check it out."

We looked around the dining room until I asked, "Were there any battles around here in the Civil War?".

"General Grant captured Paducah, about fifty miles from here, in 1862," Doc said. "That was the only major battle in the state. There were raids by both sides, especially in places like this, close to the Tennessee border, but nothing significant."

"If somebody was killed in a raid," Kendra said, "it would be significant to them and their family."

"You're right," Doc said. "Just because an event doesn't involve a lot of people, that doesn't make it unimportant. History usually just records the big things, though."

"So Amanda probably lived a pretty ordinary life," I said.

"I imagine so," Doc said. "Hard work—hauling water, weeding the fields, feeding cattle, things like that. Barely enough to eat."

"Doesn't sound like it would make a very interesting story or article," I said. "I wouldn't want to read it."

"What sort of games did she play?" Kendra asked. "That's something people might want to read about."

"She probably had a corncob doll with a dress made from her mother's sewing scraps," Doc said. "She may have had a few dishes. Playing with hoops was popular in those days."

"They played basketball then?" I asked.

Doc laughed. "Not playing hoops. Playing *with* a hoop. You get a hoop—probably a metal one that held a barrel together—and roll it along the ground, to see how far it'll go before it falls over."

I rolled my eyes. "Boy, that sure sounds like fun."

Doc sipped his coffee and swallowed. "'Fun' wasn't the point then. By age six most children of that time had regular chores. They didn't spend a lot of time playing. Children had to become little adults as soon as possible."

"Did they play baseball then?" I asked. Kendra groaned at the question.

"Something like baseball has been played in this country since before the Revolutionary War," Doc said. "It was called 'one old cat' or 'two old cats,' depending on how many bases they had. The diamond and most of the rules we use today were established in 1845, so the game could have been played here in 1862. A lot of people thought the game was sinful, though."

"Sinful!" I said. "What's sinful about baseball?"

"It took people away from their work," Doc said. "In the 1800s people still went by the rule that you work six days and rest on the seventh. If you were playing baseball on Monday through Saturday, you weren't working. And if you played on Sunday, you were breaking the Sabbath. You also need a lot of people to play, so most people felt it was a bad influence. A few lazy fellows could distract others from their work."

"Yeah, you ol' sinner," Kendra said with a laugh.

Before I could think of a good insult about tennis the waitress brought our order.

"I'll bet Amanda would have loved a breakfast like this," Kendra said as the waitress set our plates in front of us and made sure we had plenty of butter and syrup.

"She probably didn't eat this much in a whole day," Doc said. That took some of the fun out of breakfast for me.

It was almost eight-thirty when Doc dropped us off in Kendra's driveway. "Thanks again!" we both said as we got out of the car. "See you after lunch!"

Kendra headed for her steps and I walked across the road. Neither of us moved very fast. Kendra had her crutches as an excuse. I was just stuffed.

My mom was watering the roses in front of the house. "Enjoy your breakfast?" she asked.

"Yeah, it was great! I had pancakes, eggs, bacon ..."

"I thought you didn't like breakfast. It's usually all I can do to get you to eat a bowl of cereal."

"You ought to try fixing pancakes and eggs and ..."

Mom squirted the hose at my feet and I jumped out of the way. "Oh, sure. I wouldn't get to work till noon. I'll make a deal with you. You clean up the mess and I'll make you a breakfast like that every morning."

"Come on, Mom." We both laughed at our private joke. Neither of us likes to do housework. We get it done, but any excuse is good enough for us to put it off or take a break. I headed to the house.

"I heard you say something to Professor Crisp about after lunch," Mom said. "What's that all about?"

I turned back to face her. "Oh, we're going to look for some old church records to see if we can find out anything about that little girl, Amanda, or about her family. Doc has to do some stuff in town this morning, so he's going to pick us up after lunch."

Mom turned off the hose. "Be sure Kendra's mom knows where you are. I hate summers, you know it? Having to go off and leave you alone." She walked up to me and took my hand.

I hoped Kendra wasn't watching. "Mom, I can take care of myself. And Kendra's mom is always there." I didn't tell her I actually like having some time to myself. I can read, think about things, walk down to the lake, and not have to worry about going to school with creeps like Dwayne.

"I'll call you at lunch time," Mom said. "And you call me if you need anything."

"Will you be home in time for my ball game? Five-thirty?"

"Wouldn't miss it for the world! It'll mess up the supper schedule, though. Let's just pick up something after the game. Then there won't be any dishes to wash."

I patted my bulging stomach. "After that breakfast I may not even be hungry by then." Mom hugged me, got in her car, and left for the hardware store.

As I watched her drive away I felt the knot in my stomach I always get when she goes anywhere without me. I guess it comes from my memory of the day my dad left. I was only five years old then, but I can still see my mom crying and can hear myself asking where Daddy was going. I didn't know what was happening. I just knew I was afraid. Some part of that feeling has never gone away.

Maybe it never will.

I had just gotten back in the house when the phone rang. It was my grandmother.

"Hi, Gramma." She and Grampa are my dad's parents, but they've stayed close to Mom and me, even after Dad left. They don't hear any more from him than we do. They live close enough to us that I can ride my bike over to their place. I can't stay there in the summers, though, because they both work. Mom's parents live in Cincinnati, which is kind of a long way from here, so we don't see them as much.

"Good morning, Steve. Is your mother there?"

"She just left for work."

"Oh ... Well, maybe I should just talk to you. Grampa was out early this morning to get some bread. He said he saw you and Kendra and some man in the cemetery. Was that the professor your mother told us about?"

"Yes, ma'am. Today's Amanda's birthday," I said. "We put some flowers on her grave."

"Hon, why do you keep poking around there?"

"It's just something to do. Kendra thinks there's some kind of mystery she can solve. I'm just watching her so I can say 'I told you so' when she gets tired of this detective stuff." I decided not to mention writing an article or story. That still sounded too good to believe.

"Sweetheart, why don't y'all just leave the past alone? You can't change it or do anything about it."

"Gramma, do you know something about that grave?" She didn't say anything for a minute. I wasn't sure she was still there. "Gramma?"

When she finally did say something her voice was soft, almost like she didn't want to tell me what she had to say. "When I was a little girl we used to make up stories about why that grave was off by itself. There were scary stories about that whole end of the cemetery. They're nonsense, of course, but I'm afraid if you start nosing around, we may all learn more than we want to know."

CHAPTER 8

As Doc DROVE us down to the church after lunch I said from the back seat, "I hope we don't have to talk to old Mrs. Palmer."

"Who is Mrs. Palmer?" Doc asked.

"She's the full-time secretary at our church," Kendra said. "Mrs. O'Connor's there too, but she just works two days a week."

"I wish it was the other way around," I said.

"What's wrong with Mrs. Palmer?" Doc asked, glancing at me in the rearview mirror.

I would never admit it to anybody—not even Kendra—but I had disliked Mrs. Palmer ever since I overheard her say something to my Sunday School teacher about 'that Patterson boy' not having decent clothes to wear to church. It was such a pity, she said, about his father running off. She thought the church should try to find some clothes for me if my mother couldn't buy them. I wanted to tell her my mother could afford any clothes I needed! I never would forgive Mrs. Palmer for talking about Mom and me like that.

"She's nosy," I said.

"My mom says she's interested in people," Kendra said.

"Interested or nosy?" Doc said as he parked close to the back door of the church. "Depends on how you look at it, doesn't it?"

"My mom says she's good about finding out who's in the hospital," Kendra said, "and what kind of help they need. She's had it kind of rough lately, with her husband dying."

Doc helped Kendra out of the car. "How old is she?"

"She's *real* old," I said.

"As old as I am?" Doc asked with a smile that let us know he was teasing.

"She's ... older?" I said, suddenly not so sure. "How old are you?"

"I'm fifty-five, and that sounds as ancient to me sometimes as it does to you."

We went in through the back door to the church office. When Mrs. Palmer saw Kendra on her crutches she started fussing over her like Kendra was recovering from a broken leg, not just a lousy little sprained ankle.

"Why, child, whatever did you do to yourself?" she said. "Why aren't you home in bed? Here, you sit down and put your foot up."

"I'm okay, Mrs. Palmer," Kendra said. "Really. It looks worse than it is."

Once Kendra was settled, Mrs. Palmer seemed to realize there were other people in the room.

"Steve, how are you? You look nice today."

"Thanks," I muttered.

"Mrs. Palmer," Kendra said, "this is Professor Crisp. He's a friend of ours."

"It's nice to meet you, Professor," Mrs. Palmer said. "Are you from around here?"

I studied the two of them as Mrs. Palmer offered her hand and Doc shook it. She was shorter than he was, and her hair wasn't as gray. She probably dyed it, like my grandmother in Cincinnati did hers.

"No," Doc said. "I teach history at Halley College in Indiana."

"Oh, you're a history professor?"

I wanted to say, Well, *duh*, when you teach history at a college, you're a history professor.

Doc was more polite. "Yes. I specialize in the period between the Revolutionary and Civil Wars."

Mrs. Palmer smiled really big. "That's fascinating. My late husband loved to read about the Revolution. He always wanted to travel to see the sites of some of the battles. We were saving that for retirement ..."

"Steve and Kendra told me about your loss," Doc said. "My wife died earlier this year, so I know what you're going through."

"Oh, I'm so sorry," Mrs. Palmer said. They were still shaking hands. Only I think it had turned into holding hands. "Losing someone like that changes everything, doesn't it? Things you used to do, places you used to go—they just don't feel right any more."

"That's so true. I'm down here to sell the cottage my wife

and I own on the other side of the lake. I can't bear to stay in it."

"For me it's my husband's library. He had a large collection of books about the Revolution. It makes me sad just to look at them, but I don't have the heart to get rid of them yet."

"You should have someone go through them first, to see if any of them are valuable," Doc said. "I could probably find some time to do that."

"Oh, I couldn't impose on you like that." Mrs. Palmer finally let go of Doc's hand.

"It wouldn't be any trouble," Doc assured her. "Since my wife died, I seem to have a lot of time on my hands."

They were looking at one another like they kind of understood one another. Doc was betraying me again! First he sent Kendra a book of detective stories. Now he was actually liking this horrible woman. Better not let him meet Dwayne, I thought. He'd probably adopt him.

I moved around Doc to stand next to Kendra. That seemed to bring Doc back to reality.

"Well, to get back to our reason for being here," he said. "We were wondering if this church has any old records, particularly from the 1860s."

"Old records?" Mrs. Palmer said. "Why, yes. We've got things going back to the founding of the church in 1847. The oldest records are stored in a closet in the library."

"Was the original church building on this site, where this building is now?" Doc asked.

"Yes, it's always been where it is now." Mrs. Palmer's tone struck me as almost sweet. Kendra gave me a funny look, so I knew she felt the same thing. "The sanctuary is the original building. The church has grown and been added onto a couple of times, but it's always been up here."

"Was there ever a building on the lower side of the cemetery?" Doc asked.

"Not in my lifetime."

"Have there been any church fires?" Doc continued.

"No." Mrs. Palmer led the way down the hall to the library. We passed a door leading into the sanctuary. It was open.

"I haven't seen the inside," Doc said. "May I?"

"Certainly," Mrs. Palmer said. Kendra and I followed them in.

Doc turned his head one way and another. "This is beautiful. Just beautiful."

To me it just looked like our church. The whole inside is painted white. The windows have stained glass in them, but it's just colors. There aren't any pictures of Bible scenes like some churches have in their windows.

"We're very proud of our sanctuary," Mrs. Palmer said. "It was completed in 1849 and remains unchanged, except for electricity and repainting. It's registered as a historic building."

"It's bigger than I would expect for a rural church," Doc said.

"A local farmer, George Williams, gave very generously and enabled the congregation to put up a larger building than they really needed. The church has never been very big, but these days, we're growing. With so many people vacationing here during the summer, we find ourselves a bit crowded."

"That gallery—" Doc pointed to a U-shaped balcony that runs around the sanctuary—"that was where the slaves sat?"

"Yes," Mrs. Palmer said. "Today, though, it's where the young people like to sit when their parents can trust them to behave themselves."

She gave Kendra and me one of her sick smiles. Our parents did let us sit with some of our friends in the balcony. And we did behave ourselves.

"From a symbol of slavery to a place of freedom," Doc said. "I like that. Now, about those old records."

Mrs. Palmer led us into the library and unlocked a closet. It smelled like the storage room at Gramma and Grampa Patterson's— kind of stale and old. A bunch of cardboard boxes sat on the floor.

"The really old records are in here," she said. "They run from the time the church was started up to about 1930. We're computerizing our records now, starting with the most recent and working back. Unfortunately, these are not in any order, as far as I know."

"Looks like we're all set," Doc said.

"Can I get you anything else?" Mrs. Palmer asked.

"No," Doc said. "You've been very helpful."

"I try to be," she said with a smile that almost turned my stomach. "What is it you're looking for?"

I knew it, I thought. She's so nosy she's just dying to know what we're up to.

But Doc was too smart for her. "Something we probably won't recognize until we see it."

"Well, I'll be in the office if you need anything." She left the library and Doc, Kendra, and I turned to face the closet.

"Steve," Doc said, "let's move these boxes over by that table."

The boxes weren't too heavy, so I shoved a couple of them over to the table where Kendra had sat down.

"No sense getting all of them out at once," Doc said. "They'll just get in your way."

"That's probably enough for now," Kendra said.

Doc pulled out a handkerchief and dusted off his hands. "I'd love to see what's in here, but I have to leave. The real estate agent and I have some things to talk about. Be careful with these books. They're in good shape, it looks like, but the pages will be brittle. Turn them slowly. If I can finish this real estate stuff, I'll check back later."

"Thanks, Doc," Kendra and I said. When he was out of sight, Kendra added, "It might take him a while to get out of here."

"What do you mean?"

"You saw the way they were looking at each other. I thought she was never going to let go of his hand."

"Get serious, Kendra. Doc and old lady Palmer?" Since I'd had the same suspicion, I was afraid it must be true.

"You don't hear his car starting right away, do you?" Kendra pointed out.

I looked out the window of the library. Doc hadn't even gotten to his car yet. "Well, old people act crazy sometimes."

Kendra nodded. "Sometime I'll tell you about how my grandparents celebrated their fortieth anniversary. Talk about crazy."

"That's not what we're here for," I said. "The sooner we get finished, the sooner I can go get ready for my ball game tonight."

"You and your ball games! All right, let's see what we've got here."

I did most of the digging in the boxes while Kendra sat and rested her ankle. We found the records from the 1860s and 1870s in the fourth box we opened. It held some old business ledgers, about as thick as the spiral notebooks Kendra and I use in school. A date was printed in gold on the spine of each one.

"These things are dirty," Kendra said. "Get some paper towels from the rest room so we can wipe them off. And wet a couple of them so we can wipe our hands."

When I got back with the paper towels we wiped the dust off a couple of the ledgers and examined them. Each ledger contained a year's records of the activities of the church. On the first page or two was the pastor's name and a list of all the members at the beginning of the year. Occasionally beside one of the names we found the word *obit* and a date.

"I'll bet that's the day that person died," Kendra said.

"Why do you think that?"

"Because *obit* looks like 'obituary'."

Other pages in the ledgers listed people who had joined the church, gave financial reports, notices of weddings and baptisms, and recorded the minutes of church meetings.

"This handwriting sure is hard to read," I said. "All those curlicues and the long tails on the 'p's and 'g's."

"Yeah, worse than some of the girls in our class," Kendra said.

I finally found the ledger for 1861. "We're getting close." I leaned over to put it aside.

Kendra reached for it. "Let's check it while it's out, just to see if the Allens were members before 1862." I handed it to her, and she carefully wiped the dust off the top of it.

"Are you going to read it or eat lunch off of it?" I asked.

She wrinkled her nose at me, and opened the book to look up and down the first page. I waited for her to say something, but her eyebrows just came together tightly and she stared at the page like it was written in a foreign language.

"What's the matter?" I asked.

"I don't believe this. Listen: 'The Record of the Year's Business of Williams Road Baptist Church, Trigg County, Kentucky, in the Year of our Lord 1861. Pastor, the Reverend Matthew Allen'."

CHAPTER 9

IT TOOK A MINUTE for that to sink in. "*Reverend* Matthew Allen? He was the pastor of the church?"

"That's what it says."

"Wow, we never expected that."

"And it makes it even more mysterious that his daughter is buried off by herself like that," Kendra said.

"Yeah, I guess you're right." I didn't want anything else about this business to be 'mysterious.' I wanted to be finished with it. "You wouldn't expect the minister's daughter to be stuck off in the corner that way. Are his wife and Amanda mentioned in the members' list?"

"Yeah, here they are."

We flipped through the rest of that volume but didn't find anything else interesting. In the minutes of the church's summer meeting there was a mention of several young men going off to Tennessee to join the army.

"The Civil War started in April of that year, didn't it?" Kendra said.

"Wars always used to start in April," I said. "Remember what Mr. Sumner told us? They couldn't fight until the weather got warm and the ground dried out."

I dug back into the box. "Hey, here's the volume from 1860 and—*ta da!*—the one from 1862."

"Let's look at 1860 first," Kendra suggested, "to see when Mr. Allen became pastor. He was already here at the beginning of 1861, so he must have come in 1860."

We didn't have to look far. The ledger for 1860 contained another minister's name with the notice '*obit* Apr. 17th' beside it. The minutes of the church meetings showed that Reverend Allen arrived in July to become the new pastor. He and his family were greeted at a reception on July 8th, after he preached his first sermon. The secretary recorded that they had purchased the forty acres of the Williams farm nearest the church.

"But it doesn't say where it is," I said.

"I guess everybody back then would have known," Kendra said. "It must have been pretty close around here, though, if it was the forty acres nearest the church."

"It's going to be hard to remember all this stuff. It's time for my trusty ol' notebook." From the back pocket of my jeans I pulled out the small notebook with a stub of a pencil stuck in the spiral wire.

"Hey, you can be Dr. Watson," Kendra said as I flipped to a new page.

I had no clue what that meant. I probably looked like it.

"He's the guy who wrote down Sherlock Holmes' cases."

"Oh." I didn't want this to be a 'case,' so across the top of a page I wrote 'The Secret of the Lonely Grave.' I liked that better as a title for a story. Then we listed everything we knew about the Allens so far. It wasn't much.

We pulled out the 1862 ledger. Reverend Allen's name was still on the first page as pastor, but there was a line drawn through it and beside it somebody had written '*Resig. Aug 14th*'. Another minister's name appeared below Reverend Allen's.

"I'll bet that means '*Resigned August 14th*'," Kendra said so I added that to our list of facts.

"I wonder why they crossed out his name," Kendra said. "They didn't do that with any of the people who died."

"It makes it look like they're mad at him."

"Oh, yeah! Like if you write a friend's name on your notebook and then get mad at them, you scratch it out." Her hand scrubbed out an imaginary word in the air.

"I wonder what could have gotten the people in the church so ticked off at him?"

Turning the yellowed pages carefully, we finally found the minutes of a church meeting held on August 13. We helped each other figure out the flowery old handwriting, and guessed at some spots where the ink had faded:

The congregational meeting was called to order at 7 p. m. on Wednesday, August 13th, 1862, by Arthur Morris, chairman of the Board of Deacons. Deacon Morris reported that Rev. Allen had been asked to resign, following a meeting of the Board of Deacons on the 12th of this month. Rev. Allen has refused to submit his resignation. A motion was made by Deacon Ezra Clay and seconded by Thomas Pendergrass that Rev. Allen be removed as pastor of the church, effective immediately.

"Ezra Clay? Is he an ancestor of yours?" Kendra asked.

"I don't know. We could ask Gramma." My grandmother's name was Clay before she got married, and my middle name is Clay, like my dad's.

"It would be pretty cool if it was," Kendra said. "We won't find any of my ancestors in here. They had to sit in the balcony, and you know they didn't have a say in any church meetings."

"At least we've made some progress since then," I said.

"Yeah, some." She turned back to the ledger and we continued to read:

After lengthy discussion the motion was carried by a vote of 47 to 11. Deacon Clay then moved that Rev. Allen's name be stricken from the church register. The motion was seconded by Alfred MacDonald and carried by a vote of 47 to 11. There being no further business to hand, the meeting was adjourned at 9:20 p. m.

"Looks like they were really mad about something," I said.

"Excuse me," Mrs. Palmer said, sticking her head in the library door. "It's four o'clock, time for me to leave. I'll have to ask y'all to put that stuff up now."

"We will," Kendra said. "Thank you for letting us look at it."

Following Kendra's orders, I put the 1862 book on top of one box and set that box in front of the closet. "That way we can find it easily when we come back."

"Come back? Why do we have to come back?" I closed the door and pulled on the doorknob to be sure it was locked.

"I don't think we've learned all we can from these books."

When we walked past the office we found Doc talking to Mrs. Palmer. I wondered if he'd ever left. "Did you find what you were looking for?" she asked.

"We found some interesting stuff," Kendra said.

"Good! I've been thinking about some things I used to hear when I was a little girl. My grandmother told me stories about that plot of land below the cemetery being haunted. She probably just didn't want me playing there. People also used to call that big old maple tree the Judas Tree. But it's been years since I heard anybody use that name."

CHAPTER 10

I BLINKED AS we came out into the sunlight. The day had turned out warm. Mrs. Palmer locked the door and fumbled in her purse for her sunglasses. I checked my watch. "Man, I didn't realize we were in there so long. I need to get warmed up for the game."

"What time do you play?" Doc asked.

"Five-thirty."

"Would you mind if I came?"

"That would be great."

He turned to Mrs. Palmer. "Leona, this may be too forward, but would you like to watch Steve's game with me and have dinner afterwards?"

"That sounds lovely," Mrs. Palmer said.

It sounded awful to me. I didn't want old lady Palmer watching my game. "I need to get home and warm up," I said.

"Well, go ahead," Kendra said. "You don't have to wait on me. Doc, can I have a ride? These crutches make it really hard to get up that hill."

"Sure," Doc said, but he sounded like grown-ups do when they're not really listening to you. "Steve, do you have somebody to throw to?"

"I just throw against the steps. My mom plays with me some, and sometimes Kendra does. But you know how girls throw."

"How *do* girls throw, Steve?" Mrs. Palmer asked. "I read about a girl who pitched a perfect game in Little League in New York. She struck out all eighteen batters. All of them boys."

How would she know something like that? I said, "Do you ... like baseball?"

"Very much. My husband played in the minor leagues, and both of my sons played all the way through school. I've watched hundreds of games."

Doc put a hand on my shoulder. "Girls can be good ballplayers. One team in my softball league had a young woman pitcher. She struck me out three times in one game. Let me drop Kendra off and pick up a glove and I'll be at your house as soon as I can."

Mrs. Palmer got out her car keys. "I'll give Kendra a ride. That might save you some time."

"Great," Doc said. "I'll pick you up just before five-thirty."

"You don't have to do that," Mrs. Palmer said. "My house is only two blocks from the field. I'll walk over and meet you there."

⤝ ☙❧ ⤞

I was standing in my front yard, pounding a ball into my glove and tossing up a pop fly or two when Doc drove up.

"I thought you'd be here sooner," I said, glancing at my watch. "Did you have trouble finding your glove?"

"Actually I had to go buy one." Doc pulled out a bag from the hardware store where my mom works. "My old glove's in Indiana. Never hurts to have a spare, I guess. Nice uniform."

I looked down at my red t-shirt with the white number 10 on it. "The teams in our league are named after birds and animals. We're the Cardinals."

Doc slipped the glove onto his hand, flexed it and pounded his fist into the pocket a few times. "Okay, let's throw a few. Take it easy on me. I haven't picked up a ball in five years."

I went to the worn place in the middle of the yard where I stand to throw against the steps. My mom has given up trying to get grass to grow there. Doc stood at the edge of the yard by the driveway and we swapped a few tosses. I liked the feel of the ball popping into my glove when Doc threw it. My mom tries to do things like this with me, to make up for my dad not being there, but I never feel comfortable playing ball with her. Kendra's more athletic than my mom, but she's used to hitting a ball with a tennis racket, not catching and throwing it. It felt good to just "rear back and fire," like the announcers say on the ball games on TV.

Doc returned a throw. "You do a good job of keeping the ball low."

"I have to when I'm throwing against the steps with my tennis ball. If I throw it too high it bounces back against the screen door. Mom said if I make another hole in the screen it'll come out of my allowance."

"Do you pitch for your team?"

"No, I play second base. I'm not too good at it, so I only play a couple of innings. Unless it's a close game, then I sit on the bench."

"Have you ever tried to pitch, or asked the coach if you could?"

"No. Our pitcher is this big, strong kid named Erik. He throws the ball hard, but half the time he can't get it over the plate. Coach keeps saying 'Give him a chance,' but he walks a couple of guys every inning."

"Is he the coach's son?"

"Worse. His dad sponsors the team and buys the uniforms. And he owns the hardware store where my mom works." I turned around so Doc could see the store's name on the back of my shirt.

"Couldn't you ask the coach to watch you pitch, at least in batting practice? I was an outfielder, and not a very good one, until one day our regular pitcher didn't show up for practice. I volunteered, and the rest is history, as we say in my profession. Sometimes you have to go after what you want."

"No, we can't criticize Erik. I don't think he really likes to pitch, though. His dad just told Coach on the first day of practice that Erik was a pitcher. Now he has to try to make his dad happy. Shoot, if my dad was here, I'd catch or play first base or whatever he wanted me to."

"Do you mind if I ask what happened to your dad?"

"No, it's okay. He worked for a radio station in Cadiz. One day, Mom says, he decided he was wasting his life working at a station where the daily farm report was the highest-rated show, so he left and went to Atlanta."

"Your mom didn't want to go?"

"He didn't ask her to, she said."

Doc nodded like he understood. "How often do you see him?"

"Last time I saw him, I was eight. He sends presents for Christmas and my birthday. Sometimes. Hey, here comes my mom."

Doc stepped out of the way as she pulled the car into the driveway.

"Gosh, we need to get to the ballpark." I really don't like being late to places. I'm usually the first one to get somewhere, or I would be if I could get my mom to move as fast as I wanted her to. She says I was born two weeks early and I've been trying to stay ahead ever since.

Mom looked at Doc like she was sort of surprised and thought something was funny at the same time. "So, that's what you wanted the glove for. I saw you buying it. If I'd known you were coming over here with it, I would have given you my manager's discount."

"You've got a good ballplayer here," Doc said, "and a neat kid. He reminds me of what I missed, not having children of my own. You're very lucky."

"Yes, I know, in spite of everything." Mom sounded a little sad. Then she clapped her hands. "Well, sport, we'd better get over to the field."

≪∞ଓଛୠ∞≫

"Okay, guys! Y'all listen up!" Coach Mackey shouted as we crowded around him. "The startin' line-up is posted by the bench. See where you'll be playin' and get to your positions. Mark, you're catchin'. You and Erik warm up on the sidelines."

Mark rolled his eyes. None of us like catching because we never know where Erik's wild pitches are going. And since so many runners get on base for the other team, there are a lot of plays at the plate. Catching for Erik means taking a beating. But if we want to play, we have to do what the coach says, so Mark put on the catcher's pads and mask.

I checked the line-up card just to see if my name was there—hey, miracles can happen—and then took a seat on the bench with the other subs. Glancing over my shoulder, I saw Doc and Mrs. Palmer come in. Mrs. Palmer sat on the bleachers with Mom. Doc gave me a quick wave as he came over to where Coach Mackey was watching infielders throw a ball around. They were close enough so I could hear what they said.

"Good afternoon," Doc said.

"Hi," Coach grunted, barely looking up from his clipboard.

Doc stuck his hand out. "I'm Doc Crisp, a friend of the Pattersons."

"Bill Mackey," Coach said, actually looking at Doc for the first time.

"Do you have anybody to help with the team?"

"Wish I did. Coupla the dads say they're willin' to, but somehow they never seem to get out here till the game's already started."

"I could help out," Doc said. "Hit some balls to the infield."

Coach looked a lot happier. "That'd be a big help. Then I could hit some flies to the outfield. They really need the practice."

Doc picked up a bat and spent several minutes hitting ground balls to the infielders and giving them some pointers on fielding. Coach Mackey thinks if he tells us where to stand and hits the ball to us, we'll figure out how to catch it. Maybe that's why we haven't won a game yet. Doc kept reminding the guys, "Go down on one knee, keep the glove down, make sure the ball stays in front of you."

Then he turned to the bench and said, "Steve, come out here and throw me a few, so we can get the feel of a game."

I looked at him like he was speaking a foreign language. When he said it again, I picked up my glove and scrambled out of the dugout, almost tripping over a bat.

Doc tossed me a ball. "Don't make any holes in the screen," he said.

Miguel, who had been taking throws from the infielders for Doc, put on a catcher's mask and crouched behind the plate. Doc stepped into the batter's box. I concentrated on the catcher's glove, trying to imagine where the bottom step would be.

My first pitch was up around Doc's waist. "Top step," he said, shaking his head. The guys in the infield looked at one another, like they were wondering what he was talking about.

I took a deep breath. My next three pitches were down around Doc's knees. He hit ground balls to different infielders. As I turned back to face home plate after watching the second baseman scoop up a grounder and toss to first, I glanced at Doc. He gave me a quick smile and thumbs-up sign.

"Here, Miguel," Doc said as the first baseman threw the ball back to me, "give me your glove and you hit a few."

Miguel bats third in our line-up, and he's a pretty good hitter, but I threw three pitches right at his knees. He managed to tap the last one weakly to first.

Chris, one of my fellow subs, batted next. As he put his helmet on I noticed Kendra and her parents taking their seats in the bleachers. Kendra waved and smiled. I barely nodded my head to her. Then I reared back and fired the ball as hard as I could—over Chris, over Doc, and all the way to the backstop.

Doc picked the ball up and trotted out to the mound. We turned our backs on home plate. "So much for that screen door," he said as he flipped the ball to me. "Now you know how *not* to pitch. You were doing great. You don't have to throw hard. Just throw strikes. Bottom step."

When we turned back toward home plate Erik had taken Chris' place in the batter's box. He was swinging his bat like a club, daring me to throw the ball past *him*.

Doc crouched behind the plate and held the glove low to give me a target. I decided to make my first pitch one nobody would expect—a change-up. I started my pitching motion like I was going to throw at regular speed, but at the last instant I slowed up, so the ball almost floated up to the plate. Erik was so fooled by the pitch he was already through his swing by the time the ball got to him. He looked silly and everyone on the field knew it, but no one dared to laugh.

Erik gripped the bat tighter. My next pitch was full speed and barely over his shoetops, a lot lower than I intended. But Erik was so determined to knock this one over the fence, he was going to swing, no matter what. The force of his swing knocked him off his feet and sent his batting helmet flying.

As Doc threw the ball back to me, Kendra yelled from the stands, "Strike two!"

Erik jammed his helmet back in place, dusted off his pants, and sneered at me. "Come on! Throw me a real pitch! You got nothin' but junk!"

I could tell he'd decided to wait for one he could hit out of sight. My next pitch was over the inside corner of the plate and just inches above his knees. Too late, he realized it was a strike. The bat jerked helplessly on his shoulder. The infielders behind me yelled, "Strike three!"

Coach Mackey called us off the field so the other team could have time to warm up. "Thanks for helpin' me out," he said to Doc. "Would you coach first base when we bat?"

I sat on the bench. I still couldn't believe I had actually been able to pitch with guys batting. Somebody punched me between the shoulders, just hard enough to hurt but not so hard I could complain without being called a sissy. I didn't have to look to know who it was.

"Hi, ho, Steverino! So you're a battin' practice pitcher, huh?"

I stood up and faced Dwayne, keeping the bench between us. He was wearing the dark blue shirt of the Blue Jays, the team we were playing today. The right corner of his mouth was turned up in his usual sneer. But all I could see was a scared kid ducking a blow from his father. It was hard to hate Dwayne now.

"Hey, Dwayne," I said. I couldn't really be friendly to him, but I wanted to say something that wasn't just our usual exchange of insults. Dwayne didn't need somebody else giving him a hard time. "How's your team doing so far?"

"We're undefeated, Steverino, and we'll still be undefeated after this game." He jabbed a finger into my chest to emphasize the point. "I hope we'll see you out there on the mound."

"Erik's our pitcher. I play second."

"Oh, that's right," Dwayne said, like he'd forgotten. "You just pitch battin' practice. If we don't get too tired from pulverizin' Erik, maybe you can throw a little battin' practice for us."

The umpire signaled for the two teams to get ready to start the game. Dwayne headed for the other team's dugout, looking over his shoulder to throw one more insult back at me. Kendra shifted her crutches slightly, sticking one out and tripping Dwayne. He bounced up and looked around for somebody to punch. The somebody turned out to be a girl on crutches, but that wasn't what stopped him. What stopped him was that she was sitting with her father and mother.

"Sorry," Kendra said sweetly. "I didn't realize they were sticking out in your way."

By the end of the third inning we were losing 10-2. Erik had walked eight batters, thrown four wild pitches, and struck out four. As my team came to bat in the top of the fourth inning Coach Mackey motioned for Doc to step away from the bench with him. But their voices carried more than they realized.

"You really think Steve could pitch in a game?" I heard Coach ask Doc. A knot started to form in my stomach.

"What have you got to lose?"

"My best hitter, if I take Erik out. The score would be 10-0 if it wasn't for his home run. And his dad does like to see him play in that uniform he paid for."

"Coach, you don't have to be a child psychologist to see what's going on here," Doc said. "Erik's dad is pushing him to do something the boy just can't do, so they're both unhappy. The dad's yelling at Erik, at you, at the umps, since the game started. Erik snaps everybody's head off if they just look at him wrong. It's not fair to him or the whole team to make him pitch."

"Yeah, I can see all that, but that still doesn't tell me what to do about it."

"Why not try Erik at first base? He catches the ball well. He made a great play on that line drive in the second inning. Throwing the ball over the plate is his problem."

Coach rubbed his chin as he muttered, "Well, like you say, what've I got to lose?"

✥ C3 80 ઐ

I clutched my glove to my chest as I drifted off to sleep that night, with the last four innings of the game replaying in my head, like they had been doing all evening.

But this time something was different. The colors I saw were brown and that brownish orange you see in old pictures, like the ones in the baseball history book Doc gave me. I was standing on the mound again, wearing wool pants that ended at my knees, with long socks and a short-billed cap. All my teammates were dressed like me. Erik, at first base, wore suspenders and a shirt without a collar. The umpire had a thick handlebar mustache and was wearing a black suit.

In the dream I knew things were different, but knowing that didn't scare me. I felt like a time-traveler in a movie who doesn't tell the people around him what he knows. I was there to pitch my team out of trouble. Nineteenth century or twenty-first—it didn't matter.

I popped the ball into my glove, waiting for the first batter to come to the plate. The ball was brown and scuffed. It looked as bad as one I left out in the rain overnight last summer. My glove was flat, shapeless, like the glove my grandfather had shown me.

There weren't any bleachers, so people were standing around the field. Some sat in the backs of their wagons, while the horses munched from their feedbags. The men wore dark suits and had mustaches. The women wore long dresses and hats or bonnets. A few people drove by, shaking their heads and scowling. "You young wastrels!" I heard somebody shout.

Kendra waved encouragement at me. She stood next to her mother and father, wearing a long dress. Mrs. Jordan kept trying to get her to put her sunbonnet up and tie the ribbon tightly under her chin, to be ladylike. Kendra rolled her eyes the way she does when she's disgusted with something. One part of my brain knew that, because they were black, they wouldn't have been standing there with everybody else in 1862, but another part of my brain said it was *my* dream, so I could have it any way I wanted. I also knew that pitchers used to throw underhand in 1862, but I was going to throw the way I had that afternoon.

My mom stood next to Mrs. Jordan. Her clothes looked worn and her hands were red from work. She looked tired, the way she usually does by Friday night.

On the edge of the crowd stood a little girl. Her sunbonnet shaded her face so I couldn't see it. But I knew it was Amanda. She seemed to be standing with a man and a woman, but other people were in the way, so I couldn't make them out.

I had to concentrate on the batter. He stood at the plate— and it really was a tin plate. It'll be tough to hit the corners, I told myself. Nobody else there would have gotten the joke. The bases were flour sacks filled with dirt and held in place by stakes driven into the ground flush with the top of the bag. The batter waved a bat that looked like an axe handle.

It doesn't matter how big his bat is, I thought. *He's not going to hit the ball.*

The action in my dream followed what had happened in the game. I could see and feel every pitch, even the first one that bounced in the dirt in front of the plate. That made Erik's father yell, "Put the *real* pitcher back in!" Dwayne led the booing from his team's bench.

But the next three pitches were strikes. The batter looked at the first two, then swung at the third one and missed. The next two batters were also easy outs.

That one inning changed everything for my team. We started getting hits and scoring runs. In the top of the last inning Erik hit his third homer of the game, with two guys on, making the score 11-10.

When Dwayne's team came up in the bottom of the inning, the first batter hit a double. I knew I was getting tired, but I was going to finish that game. The next batter hit a high fly to right, and Miguel caught it easily. The batter was out, but the runner moved to third. I struck the next guy out.

That brought Dwayne to the plate with two out. More than anything in the world, I wanted to get him out. Not because I hated him. I didn't want to hurt or humiliate Dwayne any more. If Kendra had been standing there, I would have done anything to get her out. Winning the game was all that mattered.

Dwayne had hit a single his last time up. I had to make sure he didn't get the ball out of the infield this time. That tying run was going to stay on third.

On the second pitch Dwayne hit a slow grounder between the mound and first. I scrambled over and scooped up the ball in my glove. But Erik was also charging toward the ball. I was amazed at how fast my brain figured everything out. I knew Erik couldn't change direction and get back to first in time to take a throw. And it was too late to throw to the catcher and try to tag the runner coming in from third. My own momentum was taking me away from the plate.

So I kept running toward first and beat Dwayne to the bag by a full step. When the umpire yelled "Out!" my teammates mobbed me. It felt like the seventh game of the World Series, not just our first win of the season. Erik grabbed me in a bear hug.

As they carried me off the field I tried to see the little girl, but she turned and was walking away with the man and the woman.

No, that wasn't it. They weren't getting farther away. They were fading.

CHAPTER 11

"**HOW'S YOUR ARM** this morning?" Mom asked as I stumbled into the kitchen for breakfast.

"Pretty good."

"It's not sore?" She rubbed the upper part of my arm. "You're not used to throwing that hard for that long."

"I'm okay." I could feel some muscles I'd never felt before, but my arm didn't really hurt. It just felt kind of stiff, like I'd slept on it wrong. And I had slept later than usual. Mom likes me to be up before she leaves for work, and I like to eat breakfast with her. Today she had already finished her breakfast.

"What are you going to do today?" she asked.

"I guess Kendra will want to go back to the church and look at those old books we looked at yesterday."

"Did you find anything interesting?"

"We read about this one guy, Ezra Clay. He was a deacon in the church in 1862." I poured milk on my cereal. "Could he be some ancestor of mine?"

"He could very well be. I'm sure your grandmother would know." Mom rinsed her dishes and put them in the dishwasher.

I dug my spoon into the cereal. "I hate to say anything about this to Gramma. She keeps saying we shouldn't be poking around down there. She says we might be sorry about what we find out. This stuff happened so long ago. What difference does it make now?"

Mom poured me some orange juice and put the milk in the fridge. "Your grandmother has done a lot of research into her family's history. Not everything that happened in a family's past is always good. One of my great-grandfathers ended up in jail."

I had never heard anything about that. "What for?"

"He stole a horse. I have to finish getting ready for work."

By the time Mom had put on her make-up and brushed her teeth I was done with breakfast. She got her keys off the hook by the back door and leaned down to kiss me. "I'll talk to you at lunch. Call me if you need me."

After the garage door closed I got dressed and thought about what I was going to do. I didn't want to throw against the steps. Pitchers are supposed to rest their arms the day after a game and start throwing, but not hard, the day after that. And it looked like I was going to be a pitcher, not a second baseman. I decided to go through my baseball cards and pull out some pitchers and see what I could learn about them.

I had just started when the doorbell rang. It was Kendra. She walked into the house like a normal person, then leaned against the wall as I closed the door. Her face showed how much pain she was in.

"This ankle is *killing* me," she said. "I wasn't sure I would make it over here."

"Where are your crutches?"

"I convinced my mom I don't need them. I told her I've had enough RICE."

"But you can barely walk."

She limped over to a chair. "I hate hobbling on those things. It takes me forever to get anywhere, and I keep stumbling over stuff. I almost squashed Clyde this morning." She rested her ankle on her other knee to tighten the bandage. "I wrapped it good. That ought to be enough. I want to get back to my tennis lessons."

"If you don't use the crutches, it'll take it longer to heal."

Kendra stopped rubbing her ankle and glared at me. "Did my mother pay you to say that?"

"Hey, I don't want you to be limping around for the rest of your life."

"I may not live that long if I trip over the footstool in our den one more time. I'm not using the crutches, so don't try to make me."

"Okay, but I'm not going to carry you around."

"Nobody asked you to."

"Good."

"But you can ride me on your bike, can't you?"

Man, I stepped right into that. "Where do you want to go?"

"Down to the church. I'll keep my foot up while I'm sitting in the library."

Great. More dusty old books. I checked my watch. "It won't be open till nine. That's another twenty minutes."

"I know. I want to visit Amanda's grave first."

~ഈ ❦ ~

With Kendra's arms wrapped around my waist, I turned my bike into the church parking lot and then onto the grass and into the cemetery. For the first time that I could remember, we didn't pay any attention to Moniqa's grave. Kendra squealed and grabbed me tight when I coasted down the bumpy hill between the rows of graves. My bike's not a dirt bike or mountain bike. It likes paved roads.

"Hey, Doc's already there," Kendra said over my shoulder.

I managed to stop the bike without crashing into a tombstone.

"What's up, Doc?" Kendra called. She sounded like Bugs Bunny talking to Elmer Fudd, but Doc didn't seem to mind. I guess he's heard that all his life.

"I'm puzzled about some things," Doc said.

"What things?"

He waved his hand at Amanda's grave and the hedge beside the cemetery. "The way things are arranged here seems odd. I'd like to know who owns the vacant land behind the cemetery and when this hedge was planted. And this big tree—"

"The one Mrs. Palmer called the Judas Tree," Kendra said.

"Exactly. It stands by itself, and it's the kind of shade tree someone might have planted on the south side of a house. Or someone might have built a house near it to take advantage of the shade. I think it's old enough that it would have been good-sized when Amanda was alive."

"But there's never been a house here," I said. "That's what Mrs. Palmer told us."

"Not as far back as anyone can remember," Doc said. "You're right. But people can remember only so far back. Then you have to start digging into old records. Maybe even dig into the ground."

"You mean like an excavation?" Kendra hopped on her sore ankle. "Could we do that? Ow!"

"Whoa! Slow down," Doc said. "We'd have to get permission from the church and from somebody in the state government, probably. If the church is a registered historic building, you don't just pick up a shovel and start digging around it."

"And what if we dug up somebody's grave, one that doesn't have a marker?" I said. Just thinking about it made me shudder. I watch creepy movies, but I don't know what I would do if I actually ran into a dead body or a skeleton.

"That is another thing to consider," Doc said. "And I don't know that there's anything here to dig up. What did you find in the church records?"

We'd been so busy with my ball game yesterday and his date with Mrs. Palmer that we hadn't told him what we'd learned about Reverend Allen. His eyebrows went up when he heard.

"Pastor of the church? And they forced him out?" He glanced at Amanda's grave. "That raises a lot more questions, doesn't it?"

"It does for me," Kendra said. "And I think the answers are in those ledgers in the library. Let's get up to the church."

She sat on my bike and Doc and I pushed her up the hill, one of us on each side. Just as we got to the back door Mrs. Palmer pulled into the parking lot. Doc opened the car door for her.

"Good morning, David," she said. "And thank you again for dinner last night. I had a lovely time."

"I enjoyed it, too," Doc said. "Do you still want me to come over and look at your husband's books tonight?"

"If you have time, I would really appreciate it. Why don't you come over for dinner? About six?"

"That sounds great."

I felt kind of sick, just watching them look at one another. They reminded me of this teenaged babysitter I had one time. She invited her boyfriend over and gave me a dollar not to tell Mom. But Mom found out anyway.

Kendra got off my bike and said, "Speaking of books ..."

I think Mrs. Palmer had forgotten we were there. "Oh, I'm sorry. Why, of course. You want to get back in the library, don't you?" She got out her keys and unlocked the back door of the church. We followed her down the hall to the library.

"I'll help you get the boxes out," Doc said. "Then I have to go over to my cottage. The realtor's got a prospective buyer, but he wants some repairs made. I need to see how much I can do and what I'll have to hire somebody to do."

"I'll help them any way I can," Mrs. Palmer said.

"That's all right," Kendra said quickly. "We can manage on our own, can't we, Steve?"

I nodded.

As Mrs. Palmer and Doc started back down the hall I heard her say, "I'm going to start some coffee. Would you like a cup, David?"

"That would be nice," Doc said.

"I guess those repairs on his cottage aren't *too* urgent," Kendra said with a laugh.

Kendra got settled at a table while I pulled out the 1862 ledger. We opened it to where we had quit last time. I started to turn the page, but Kendra stopped me.

"We need to look at everything carefully," she said. "They might say something about the Allens while they're talking about something else in a meeting."

"Come on! It'll take us all day to go through the book if we read every word."

"At least it's air-conditioned in here, and you didn't want me walking around."

I snorted. "I don't have a sprained ankle, and I'm not bouncing around on it, pretending I don't need crutches. It's summer. I want to be outside."

"Let's do this one ledger," Kendra said. "If we don't find something about the Allens, we'll go do whatever you want to do. Maybe we'll go see if Dwayne wants to play."

I got out my notebook and sat down hard in the chair next to her. "What do you mean by 'something about the Allens'?" I've learned I have to be *very* sure what I'm agreeing to when I make a deal with Kendra.

"I mean anything that gives us a clue about what happened to them or why Amanda is buried where she is."

"So, not just seeing their name?"

"No. It has to be something important."

"What do you mean by 'important'?"

"We'll know that when we see it."

It was all I was going to get out of her. We read a few more pages of the ledger. The church had a bunch of meetings in August and September. They had to find a new pastor. A Reverend Rogers from Paducah "accepted the call" and arrived in the middle of September. Then there was a lot of debate about how much the church should support families whose men went to fight in the Civil War and whether it made any difference which side they fought on.

"Whoever made these notes was a pretty good writer," I said. "I can almost imagine being at some of these meetings."

"Ezra Clay sure had a lot to say. And he really favored the Confederates. Did you ask your grandmother if he's one of your ancestors?"

"I will the next time I see her."

"I wonder if any of *your* ancestors owned any of *my* ancestors as slaves. Would that make you feel weird?"

I shrugged. "Those people weren't us. That all happened a long time ago. Even if people in the past did things we think are wrong today, we can't go back and change anything."

"Then maybe we ought to try to make up for it. You know, do something good for people who were mistreated."

"How can we? We can't fix everything wrong that happened in the past." We couldn't even make up for my dad leaving or Dwayne getting hit by his dad.

"So we shouldn't even try?" Kendra asked.

"Remember what Mr. Sumner said in our social studies class: 'You can't change the *past*, but if you work hard in the *present*, you can make a difference in the *future*'."

Kendra nodded. "I guess you're right." But I knew I hadn't convinced her. When she can't win an argument, she acts like it isn't important any more. I turned a page in the ledger, just so we could get through and get out of there.

The next page of the ledger had a thick black line drawn around the edge and a list of fourteen names, each one followed by *obit* and a date in the middle of October.

Kendra ran her finger around the line. "That's weird. Why did all those people die at the same time?"

"Look," I said, "over here." The writing on the page opposite the list of names had faded so bad we could barely read it:

These are our brothers and sisters who died in the outbreak of influenza which decimated our area in the fall.

"What's 'decimated'?" I asked.

"I don't know," Kendra said, "but with all those people dead, I bet it's pretty bad."

"There's a dictionary over there. Hang on." I found the word. "It means 'to take a tenth part of'."

"Oh, like 'decimal'."

"Yeah, but it also means 'to destroy a large part of'."

"I guess that's what it means here. Doc was right then. All those tombstones from that one month were probably the result of some disease. What's 'influenza'?"

I found that in the dictionary. "It's a fancy name for flu."

"I wonder if that's what Amanda died from?"

"I'd bet on it." I read the list of names again. There was a Jonathan Clay. He was eleven. I pointed his name out to Kendra.

"He could be some relative of yours," she said. "It's sad to think of him dying when he was eleven."

"Sad? Shoot, it's creepy." I wrote Jonathan's name in my notebook with the date of his death. Then I studied the list some more. "There's one name that isn't here. Have you noticed?"

"It's hard to notice something that isn't there."

"Do you see Amanda's name?"

"Hey, you're right. But that's no surprise," Kendra said. "Think about it. After they forced her father to resign as pastor of the church, why would the Allens hang around?"

"But they did hang around, at least until October. That's why Amanda is buried here. And she died during this flu epidemic."

Kendra scrunched up her face the way she does when she's thinking. "Yeah, I guess you're right. So, what were they doing between the time Reverend Allen was kicked out and the time Amanda died?"

"They bought a farm when they came here. Maybe they were farming. Can we go now? We haven't found out anything else about the Allens."

"But we haven't finished going through the book. That was the deal."

"All right, all right." I flipped the page over too hard. We heard it tear.

"Watch it, Steve!" Kendra pulled my hand off the book. "If we mess something up, Mrs. Palmer won't let us back in here."

"It's not bad. Just right down there at the bottom."

"Well, be more careful." She looked around like there might be somebody else in the library to see what had happened.

We turned another page and found the minutes of another meeting of the deacons. The name 'Allen' almost jumped off the page at us. But it was Mrs. Allen.

"What was she doing there?" Kendra said. "I didn't think they let women speak at meetings in those days."

> *Ezra Clay, acting chairman of the board of deacons, ordered Mrs. Allen to leave. She refused to allow herself to be escorted from the meeting and Deacon George Williams prevented anyone from forcing her to leave. At the urging of Deacon Williams, the deacons decided to hear her out, to avoid any further unpleasantness.*
>
> *Mrs. Allen asked for permission to bury her daughter Amanda in the church cemetery. She maintained that, even though her husband was no longer pastor, she was still a member of the church. Deacon Clay reminded Mrs. Allen that church membership, in and of itself, does not entitle anyone to the privilege of burial in the cemetery. The church has the right to deny the privilege to members not in good standing. On a motion by Deacon Clay, the deacons then voted 6 to 1 to refuse to allow Amanda Allen to be buried in the church cemetery.*

"That doesn't make any sense," Kendra said. "She *is* buried in the cemetery."

"Not according to what we just read." I got out my notebook. "Where she's buried wasn't actually *in* the cemetery."

"But how could they bury her so close to it? Wouldn't that be somebody else's property?"

"Hey, maybe it was the Allens' property!" I said.

"Yeah, part of their farm."

"Come on, let's go back there and look around." I hoped maybe she'd forget my promise to go through the whole ledger.

"Look around for what? If we found anything, we wouldn't know what it was. Besides, you agreed to finish going through this ledger."

I slumped in my chair as Kendra turned the page. The report of the same meeting continued.

> *Mrs. Allen said she knew why Deacon Clay hated her and her husband, but she couldn't understand why he would take out his resentment on their daughter. Deacon Clay responded that Mrs. Allen wasn't the only one to have lost a child in the recent epidemic. He reminded her that his own son had died of the influenza. He regretted her loss, as he did the loss of every victim of the disease, but he restated firmly that the church was under no obligation to provide space for her child's burial.*

We looked through the rest of the book as quickly as I could get Kendra to turn the pages. There wasn't anything else about the Allens.

"Okay, I kept my part of the deal." I closed the book and put it back in the box. "Now can we go?"

"I guess so. I just wish there was some way to find out more about them. What happened to them? Did they leave here?"

"If they buried Amanda on their property, I think they intended to stay." I looked back over the notes I had made.

"Maybe somebody forced them to leave."

"They would've had a hard time doing that, I think. They couldn't even make Reverend Allen resign, remember?"

"But I bet Ezra Clay did everything he could to run them off." Kendra looked me right in the eye. "I'm glad your family has gotten nicer over the years."

I didn't know what to say to that. I think my family have always been pretty nice people. I wrote a couple of things down in my notebook, especially about Jonathan Clay. It really bothered me to think about somebody my age dying from the flu. If I got the flu, I would expect to miss school for a few days, but I wouldn't be afraid that I'd die.

"Are you okay, Steve?" Kendra asked. "I didn't mean to insult your family."

"You didn't. I was just making some notes."

"That's what you do when you don't want to talk to me. You pull out that notebook. It's like you're hiding behind it."

I held up the notebook. It's barely bigger than the palm of my hand. "It's not big enough to hide behind."

Kendra pushed my hand down. "You know what I mean."

I guess I did, but I didn't want to talk about it. "What do you think Mrs. Allen meant when she said she knew why Ezra Clay hated her and her husband?"

"That's one more question for your notebook." Kendra glanced around the library. "Where else could we find information about the Allens? Or about Ezra Clay? Does your grandmother have any old family records?"

"I don't want to talk to her about this, not until I have to. She gets kind of weird whenever I mention it."

"Well, where could we find out what was going on around here then?"

"Maybe the library in Cadiz has some old newspapers," I said before I thought about it.

"Yes! Old newspapers! The town newspaper might have reported something, especially if there was a lot of talk about Reverend Allen."

Rats! I'd let myself in for another summer afternoon wasted on dusty old books. "I can't ride you into town on my bike. It's too far."

"I know that. We'll have to go with one of our parents."

"My mom can't take us until Saturday."

"That's okay. My mom's going to the beauty shop *and* the grocery store today. She can drop us off and we'll have hours to look for stuff. It'll be great."

"Oh, yeah, great. Just great."

᪥ ༄༅ ᪥

CHAPTER 12

THE PUBLIC LIBRARY in Cadiz is across the street from the school Kendra and I go to. It's small, but the librarian is friendly and will help you find whatever you need. But she couldn't help us with the old newspapers.

"We didn't have enough room to keep them here," she said. "We needed the shelf space for videos and CD's. We sent the papers to the County Historical Society. It's in that big blue house two blocks from here, just off the town square. There's a sign out front."

Because of Kendra's ankle it took us a few minutes to walk to the Historical Society. She grumbled the whole way. "Sherlock Holmes never has to run around looking for things like this. He always knows where everything is, and it's always where he says it's going to be."

"That's what's so bogus about those detective stories of yours," I said. "Real detectives have to look all over the place, and they don't always find what they're after. We'll look at those old newspapers for a couple of hours and I bet we don't find a thing about the Allens."

"I bet you we will."

"What do you want to bet?" I didn't think our parents would like for us to bet on things. But our parents probably wouldn't find out.

Kendra thought for a minute. "If we find something about them, you buy me a used paperback mystery at the bookstore. They're just a buck."

"Okay." I had three dollars in my pocket. "If I win, you buy me a one-dollar baseball card." Or, if she gave me the dollar, I could buy a four-dollar card instead of a three-dollar one.

"It's a bet." Kendra stuck her hand out and I shook it.

"But, for you to win, we find something that's actually

important," I insisted before I let go of her hand. "Something we don't already know."

Our school bus passed the Historical Society every day, but I had never paid any attention to it. I was usually too busy trying to keep away from Dwayne. The house had fancy trim around the windows and doors, like my grandparents' house. Gramma calls it 'gingerbread.' It was painted white so it stood out against the dark blue of the house.

"This is like that big doll house you used to play with," I said, "the one your grandfather built for you."

"What do you mean, *I* used to play with? You used it as headquarters for your soldier dolls."

"Those aren't dolls. They're action figures."

"Oh, yeah. I forgot. Action figures."

When we entered the house there was a lady sitting behind a desk by the front door. She was our fourth-grade teacher.

"Steve, Kendra," she said. "What a nice surprise."

"Hi, Mrs. Fisher," Kendra said. "Do you work here now?"

"I volunteer in the summer. What can I help you with?"

"The lady at the library said there are old newspapers here."

"That's right. We keep them in the reading room. Are you looking for something in particular?"

"The newspapers from about 1860 to 1862."

"So you're interested in the Civil War?"

"No, ma'am. We're trying to find out about something that happened in our church back then."

"Which church is that?"

"Williams Road Baptist Church."

"We think something happened to the pastor and his family," I said. Kendra glared at me. She clearly did not want any grown-up help on her 'case.' I just wanted to get done with this stuff and go buy a baseball card. Mrs. Fisher might be able to help us faster if she knew what we were looking for.

"Who was the pastor?"

"Reverend Matthew Allen," I said. "His daughter's buried off by herself, and we want to know what happened to her parents."

"We looked at the church records," Kendra said. "That didn't help much."

Mrs. Fisher got up from her desk and led us into a large room. It had windows that came all the way down to the floor. The shelves in the room were filled with books, magazines, and old newspapers in big bound volumes. In the middle of the room was a table that slanted up toward the middle, so you could read your book more easily, especially if it was a big one.

"The paper from that period was only a weekly with four pages in each one," Mrs. Fisher said. She pulled down three large volumes with the dates stamped in gold on the spine. "These are the years you're looking for."

We sat down at the library table and Mrs. Fisher put the three volumes of newspapers in front of us. "Look as long as you like," she said. "Just be careful turning the pages. Newspapers get dry and crumbly when they're this old. Call me if you need any help. I'm going to check on something."

When Mrs. Fisher left the room Kendra said, "Get out your notebook. When did the Allens come to the church?"

I flipped through a few pages. "They got into town in July of 1860. There was a welcoming party, after church on July 8."

Kendra opened the 1860 volume and turned to July. "The paper was published every Thursday. Here's July 12."

On page three we found an article welcoming the Allens. It said they came from eastern Kentucky and that Reverend Allen had been a miner before being called to the ministry. He had a wife and daughter.

"Hah! You owe me a book!" Kendra punched me on the shoulder, my left shoulder, fortunately.

"No, that's not important," I said. "We already knew when they got here."

"But we didn't know where he was from. And we didn't know he was a miner."

"So what?"

"It might be very important. You're just trying to get out of the bet."

Since we had that volume open, we looked through the rest of it, but there wasn't anything else about the Allens.

"I'm going to look through the 1861 volume," Kendra said.

"The whole thing?"

"We might miss something if we don't. We can just skim."

That's what we did, and we found a couple of articles that mentioned Reverend Allen. In the March 21 issue there was a story about an "altercation" between him and another man on the town square.

"What's an altercation?" I asked.

"There's a dictionary," Kendra said, pointing to a stand by one of the windows. "A big one."

I lugged the dictionary over to our table and looked up 'altercation.' "It means a fight."

"It looks like this other man, Thomas Pendergrass, didn't like what Reverend Allen was saying about freeing the slaves. They got into an argument in front of the courthouse. The sheriff had to break it up. But it wasn't really a fight because Reverend Allen wouldn't defend himself. He said he didn't believe in fighting. It says he wouldn't press charges against Mr. Pendergrass."

The article also said Reverend Allen already had a reputation for his strong opposition to slavery. Even people who didn't belong to his church were attending to hear what he might say.

"I wonder what the slaves in the balcony thought?" I said.

"Do you think anybody asked them?"

There wasn't anything else in the 1861 papers about Reverend Allen or his church. Kendra opened the 1862 volume to the first page.

"Do we have to go all the way through it?" I asked. "It'll take forever. We have to meet your mother in about an hour and I want some time to look at the baseball cards." Looking at the cards, even the ones I couldn't afford, was almost as much fun as buying one.

"Yeah, I'll need time to pick out that mystery you're going to buy me. But I don't want to miss anything important."

"We know Reverend Allen was forced to resign in August. Why don't we start looking there?"

"Okay. I guess we could always come back another time."

The first issue of the paper in August of 1862 came out on the 7th. As soon as I saw the front page I knew I was going to be buying Kendra a book. There was a letter written by Reverend Allen.

"August 7th?" Kendra said. "That was right before they kicked him out, wasn't it?"

I checked my notebook. "Yeah. They voted on the 13th and made him quit the next day."

"I wonder if this letter had anything to do with it?"

We started reading the letter, but it was hard to understand.

"He sure uses a lot of big words," Kendra said.

"You read and I'll look up any words we don't know."

Kendra began to read:

To the Editor:

Dear Sir,

   Much has been said and written recently concerning my views on the abolition of slavery ("That means doing away with it," I said) *and my opposition to the current war, in fact to any war. I feel it incumbent upon me* ("necessary"), *in light of certain misrepresentations of my views, to set them forth in writing and in no uncertain terms.*

   In the first place, I do call unequivocally ("without any doubt") *for an end to slavery. How can any nation which calls itself Christian countenance* ("approve") *the buying and selling of one human being by another? Are we not all brothers and sisters? I concede* ("admit") *that not even Jesus himself advocated* ("called for") *an end to slavery. But he lived in a society which would not have comprehended* ("understood") *such a call. Nowhere did he approve of this barbaric* ("cruel") *practice, and the love and brotherhood which he preached make it clear what he intended for his followers to do.*

   To secure the abolition of slavery I am willing to help slaves escape, should the opportunity arise, and find freedom. The book of Deuteronomy, chapter 23, specifically forbids us to return an escaped slave to his master, so I am not preaching merely my own doctrine on this point.

   I do not, however, advocate war to abolish slavery. We cannot eradicate ("get rid of") *one evil by another, greater one. Thousands of young men have already died; tens of thousands more will die, and to what avail ("use")? Slavery could be abolished overnight by Congressional action, or by a Presidential decree ("order"). A period of adjustment would be needed, I realize, but it would not be any longer or harder than the process of rebuilding which we will have to endure after this terrible war is ended.*

Kendra let out a low whistle. "Boy, he sure let you know what he thought, didn't he?"

"Yeah. He opposes slavery *and* the war. That letter probably made just about everybody in town mad."

"But, remember from history class this year," Kendra said. "On January 1, 1863, the Emancipation Proclamation freed the slaves in the Confederate states. Reverend Allen was suggesting that several months earlier." She sounded as though she was kind of proud of him.

"At least now we know why the church got rid of him. But we still don't know what happened to him and his wife."

Mrs. Fisher came back into the room. She was carrying a book with her finger stuck in it to mark her place. "Have you found anything interesting?"

"Not yet." Kendra turned the page like she didn't care what was on it and scanned the next page.

Mrs. Fisher held out the book and opened it. "This is a history of your church, written in 1947, when the church was celebrating its one-hundredth anniversary. I'm surprised someone up there hasn't shown you a copy."

"The pastor didn't really understand what we're doing," Kendra said.

"And the secretary has other things on her mind," I added.

"Here's a picture taken on the church's fifteenth anniversary, in April of 1862."

She opened the book to show us a picture of a bunch of people standing in front of our church. Most of the men had beards and wore dark, heavy-looking suits and shirts with high collars. The women looked just as uncomfortable in their long dresses and bonnets. Nobody smiled.

Mrs. Fisher pointed to one of the men. "The caption says this is the pastor, Matthew Allen."

Kendra squealed. "I don't believe it! There he is."

Reverend Allen was shorter than most of the men in the picture. He wasn't wearing a hat, and his hair and beard seemed to be a lighter color.

"I'll bet the woman next to him is his wife," Kendra said.

The woman next to Reverend Allen had her hand resting on his arm. She was pretty, even with her hair pulled back in a bun. Her dress looked like the other women's, except for a row of white buttons down the front and some lace on the cuffs.

"I think those buttons might be pearls," Mrs. Fisher said.

I pointed to a small girl standing in front of Mrs. Allen, holding her mother's skirt with one hand and squinting against the sun. "That must be Amanda."

Kendra rubbed a finger over the picture as though she could touch the people in it. "Wow, they *were* real! Look, you can tell her hair color and see how round her face was."

"Does the book tell anything about them?" I asked.

"Just what I think you already know," Mrs. Fisher said. "When they came here, his forced resignation—the person who wrote the book got the information from the same church records you've seen, I'm sure. I'll make you a copy of these pages and enlarge the picture."

"Thanks," we both said as she left the room.

"So we don't know any more than we did," Kendra said. Her shoulders slumped in disappointment.

"And we don't have a lot more time to spend here, if you want me to buy you that book I guess I owe you." I stood up and put my notebook in my pocket.

"Let's stay a little longer. We know Amanda died in October. Let's look at the papers through the end of 1862. It won't be that many. Come on, Steve."

I sighed and sat back down. I knew that tone of voice. I'd heard it when Kendra was learning how to put backspin on her serve. Blisters and sore muscles meant nothing to her. Nothing would get her out of this room except to finish looking through the stupid newspapers. I began turning pages, hardly noticing what was on them. Until a headline from November 6 caught my eye:

CONFEDERATE RAIDERS STRIKE

"Doc said there weren't any battles around here."

"A raid isn't exactly a battle," Kendra pointed out.

We read in silence. The article described how a band of Southern soldiers had come into the area looking for 'stations' on the Underground Railroad.

"When you did your report on the Underground Railroad, you didn't say anything about slaves escaping through here."

"Nobody knows exactly where every station was. It would make sense to have one here. We're just a couple of miles from the Tennessee state line. And this is the narrowest part of Kentucky. The Ohio River is a lot closer here than if they were trying to cross the eastern part of the state."

Mrs. Fisher came back in with the pages she had copied for us. Even the picture of the people in front of the church turned out pretty good. We thanked her.

"I'm glad to help," she said. "I've got some cataloguing to do, but you can stay as long as you like."

"I've already stayed longer than I like," I said as she left.

"But we found some really neat stuff. Let's just finish this article. If we have to, we can come back."

According to the article, the presence of the soldiers had frightened the local people, but there were no known injuries and no damage to property except that the raiders "burned one small house near the Baptist Church on Williams Road."

"Oh, my gosh!" Kendra said. "That's it."

"What?" I looked at the article again to see what I had missed. "What's it?"

"The house they burned. Don't you get it? Whose house was it?"

I looked back at the paper. "The article doesn't say. How would I know?"

"It's elementary, my dear Patterson," Kendra said in a fakey British accent.

"What are you talking about?"

"That's what Sherlock Holmes says when he figures out something before Dr. Watson does, which is all the time."

"Well, I'm not Dr. Whatzit and you're not Sherlock Holmes, so just tell me."

"Okay. The house that was burned must have been the Allens' house."

Kendra looked really pleased with herself while I read the article again. I still didn't see how ... "The Allens' house? Why do you think that? There could have been other houses on Williams Road."

"You read what Reverend Allen said about helping slaves escape. He'd be the perfect person to have a station on the Underground Railroad—in his house."

That made sense, I had to admit. "I wonder how the Confederates found out about it?"

"Somebody must have told them," Kendra said. "Somebody who really hated Reverend Allen."

"You mean Ezra Clay, don't you?"

"I think there's a good chance it was him."

"But what about that guy who got in a fight with Reverend Allen?" I flipped back through my notebook. "Thomas Pendergrass. He voted against Reverend Allen when they forced him to resign."

"Okay, so we have two suspects in the case."

I looked back a few more pages in my notebook. "More than that. There were forty-seven people who voted to force him to resign."

"Maybe you're right. Maybe we never will know who told the Confederates." Kendra glanced at her watch. "Hey, we'd better head for the bookstore. It always takes me a while to go through the mysteries."

"Did you find what you were looking for?" Mrs. Fisher asked as we left.

"We found some stuff," Kendra said. "Thanks for your help, and for the picture."

⊱⊰

On our way to the bookstore we passed a real estate office. A familiar car with Indiana license plates was parked out front. "Hey, that's Doc's car," I said.

"He sure has been spending a lot of time with the real estate guy," Kendra said.

"I guess that means he'll be leaving soon. You want to go over and say hi?"

"I don't want to bother him. He might be signing some papers or something. Give me a piece of paper and your pencil."

I tore a page out of my notebook. Kendra wrote AMANDA WAS A BLONDE in big letters and put the note under the windshield wiper of Doc's car.

Kendra's mother was going to pick us up at the used book store. It's one block off the main square of town. We don't like the owner, Mr. Morse. He's bald except for a fringe of white hair around his ears. He has a white beard with strands of brown and red mingled in it, so it just looks dirty. He never smiles, and he smokes all the time. But he has lots of used books, comic books, and baseball cards.

Kendra headed straight for her mysteries. The section with the baseball cards is off to one side of the store. That's where I went. I was trying to figure out what I could get since I would have a dollar less than I'd planned on. The little bell over the door jingled and I looked up without thinking about it. Then I wished I hadn't.

Dwayne Mitchell just walked in.

CHAPTER 13

I DECIDED TO forget about buying any cards. Staying behind the shelves and display cases as best I could, I worked my way around to where Kendra was.

"Hurry up! Let's get out of here," I said.

"What's the matter?"

"Look who just walked in." I led her to the end of the row of books she had been looking at and nodded toward the comic book section, where Dwayne was leafing through the collectors' comics. Each comic was in a plastic bag, and they were sorted by characters. Dwayne seemed to be a *Wonder Woman* fan.

Kendra ducked behind the books. "My mom will be here in fifteen minutes. We can stay back here out of sight until then."

"I want keep to him in sight so he can't sneak up on me."

"He doesn't even know you're here. Relax."

I took a deep breath and tried to think about something besides Dwayne. I noticed Kendra had a couple of books in her hand. "I'm only buying one, remember."

"I know. I'm trying to decide."

I couldn't stop myself from peeking around the end of the row again. Kendra looked too by craning her neck over my head. Mr. Morse had gone over to the baseball card section to help somebody. As soon as he was distracted, Dwayne slipped a comic book under his shirt.

Kendra grabbed my arm. "Steve! He's stealing a comic book. We've got to stop him."

"Why do *we* have to stop him?"

"'Cause it's not right to steal."

"It's not right for Dwayne to beat people up either, but that's what he'll do to us if we squeal on him. Let's just stay out of it. He's not hurting us. It's not our comic book."

"Well, I'm not going to stand here and let him get away with it." Kendra started toward the counter as Dwayne edged his way to the door. He was trying to look like the most innocent person in the store, so he stopped to browse at a comic or two and put them back. I grabbed Kendra's arm.

"Look, I know you're right. We can't just let somebody steal something. But let's do it this way." I took out my notebook and scribbled, 'The boy in the blue shirt is stealing a comic.' I handed the note to Kendra. "Tell Mr. Morse your mother wants a book and give him this note."

Kendra hurried over to the counter as fast as she could on her bad ankle and handed the note to Mr. Morse. I could see Dwayne hesitate when he spotted her. Then he decided to make his getaway while Mr. Morse was busy. He had his hand on the doorknob when Mr. Morse reached over the counter and clamped a hand on his shoulder.

"Hold it right there," he said. "Let me have it." He held up his other hand and wiggled his fingers.

Dwayne turned pale. I could see him scrunching up his shoulder, the way he did when his father hit him. He was shaking as he pulled the comic out of his shirt.

Mr. Morse examined the price tag. "That's two-fifty plus tax. Pay it or I call the cops."

"I ... I don't have no money." Dwayne looked at the floor. "Can't I just ... put it back?"

Mr. Morse grabbed his arm and jerked him up straighter. "This ain't no game we're playing, son. I've been missing some comics lately, and you've been coming in here a lot lately. But you never buy anything. Buy this one, or I call the cops."

Everybody else in the store had stopped what they were doing to look at Dwayne and Mr. Morse. I stepped out from my hiding place, with my hand clutching the three dollars in my pocket, and took a few steps toward the door. Then I stopped, like I was surprised.

"Hey, Dwayne, I'm glad I ran into you. I've got that three dollars I owe you." I held out the money.

"I'll take it," Mr. Morse snapped. Releasing his grip on Dwayne, he grabbed the bills. He put the money in the cash register and slammed it shut.

Dwayne looked from me to Mr. Morse like he didn't know what to do. He had been caught red-handed and somebody had been kind to him, both at the same time. Like a dog being swatted with a newspaper while somebody was patting his head, he couldn't figure which gesture to respond to. He straightened his shirt, squared his shoulders, and put that smirk back on his face.

"What about my change?" he said, picking up the comic off the counter.

"Don't press your luck, kid," Mr. Morse said. "I don't want to see you in here again unless you've got your own money in your hand. I'll be watching you every minute you're in the store, and I'm going to search you when you leave. Now, get out of here!"

He drew back his hand, as if he was about to slap Dwayne, who ran out the door and took off down the street.

"Thanks, kids," Mr. Morse said. "For helping me, I'll let you pick something for free. A book, a baseball card. Within reason, of course."

"Great!" Kendra said. She put the two paperbacks she was carrying up on the counter. "See, I can't decide which one I want to read more ..."

Mr. Morse waved his hand. "Take 'em both." He looked at me. "How about you? You like the baseball cards, don't you?"

"I don't want anything. Thanks anyway." I pushed the door open and stepped out to the sidewalk.

Kendra limped out after me. "What's wrong with you? You could have had a free baseball card."

"I just didn't feel right taking a reward for humiliating Dwayne. But you got a couple of free books. That's good."

"You still owe me one." She held up the two paperbacks. "This doesn't have anything to do with our bet."

"I know."

"Why did you give Dwayne that money? Mr. Morse was going to call the cops. That would've fixed him good. They would've called his parents. Can you imagine how mad Dwayne's dad would be when he heard Dwayne got caught shoplifting?"

"Yeah, I can. I *really* can."

"But you let him off the hook. Why?"

There was no way to explain how I felt when I saw Dwayne's father hit him. And if I couldn't make Kendra understand that, I couldn't explain what I had just done. "Look, you stopped a crime from being committed. Doesn't that satisfy the detective part of you?"

"Yeah. But you still owe me a book. And it has to be one you pay for. That was the bet."

⋞⋐ॐ⋑⋟

We sat down on a bench outside the courthouse, where we could still see the bookstore and know when Kendra's mom came to pick us up. There was no shade over the bench, and the day had gotten really hot.

"I wish I had something to drink," I said.

"You could buy yourself a drink if you hadn't given Dwayne your money. Why did you do that? Now every time he sees you, he's probably going to want money not to beat you up."

"Give it a rest, Kendra!"

I got up and walked over to the fountain in front of the courthouse. It's part of a monument put up to honor the Confederate soldiers from Cadiz. It has tall columns at the four corners and fountains on the front and back. But the fountains don't work any more, I discovered.

"They should set out a bucket of water and a drinking gourd," Kendra said, "like the song from the Underground Railroad. Do you remember that from my report?" She began to sing.

"*When the sun comes back,*
And the first quail calls,
Follow the Drinking Gourd.
For the old man is waiting
    for to carry you to freedom, if you
Follow the Drinking Gourd'."

I hope she makes it as a tennis player, because nobody would pay to listen to her sing. They might pay *not* to listen to her.

"Yeah, I remember it," I said, just to stop her from singing. "The drinking gourd is the Big Dipper. The song reminded slaves to keep the Big Dipper in front of them, so they would always be heading north when they escaped. The stations on the Underground Railroad were usually marked with a drinking gourd symbol."

I stopped, then got out my notebook. "Oh, my gosh! Oh, my gosh!"

"What? What's the matter?"

I showed her the page where I had drawn the thing that was carved on the back of Amanda's tombstone. "That's not a hand with a finger pointing out. It's a drinking gourd."

[NOTE: THE WORDS TO "FOLLOW THE DRINKING GOURD" CAN BE FOUND ON PAGE 152]

~&CʒꝚꝚ&~

CHAPTER 14

WHEN MRS. JORDAN turned the car onto Williams Road and started driving up past the cemetery, Kendra asked her if we could stop.

"What on earth for?" Mrs. Jordan asked.

"We want to look at Amanda's grave. Just for a minute."

I looked at her, puzzled. 'We'?

"Kendra, honey," her mother said, "that old grave's been there for over a hundred years. It'll be there tomorrow. We've got to get ready to go over to Hopkinsville. It's Friday night, you know."

For several years Kendra's family has been visiting a home for old people in Hopkinsville, about twenty miles east of Cadiz. Some of the people there don't have anybody to come see them. I went with them a couple of times, when my mom had to work on Friday night.

"Do I *have* to go?" Kendra asked. I could sympathize with her. It sure wasn't the most fun I'd ever had.

"You know those old folks adore you. They love to hear you sing."

Probably with their hearing aids turned off, I thought.

"But, Mom, my foot hurts a lot. I ... I guess I was walking around on it too much today."

Mrs. Jordan looked in the rearview mirror as she stopped at my driveway. She had that look on her face that parents get when they see right through your lame excuses. "That sprained ankle sure is turning into a convenient injury. It hurts when you want it to, and it doesn't when you don't want it to."

My mom had just pulled into the driveway and was almost in the front door. She turned around and came out to the car. Mrs. Jordan lowered the window on the passenger side.

"How was your afternoon?" she asked as I got out.

"Interesting," I said. Kendra nodded.

"Did you buy that baseball card you've been wanting?"

"No ... It was gone." Kendra and I had agreed we wouldn't tell anybody about me giving my money to Dwayne.

"That's too bad. But you can save up your money and get a nicer one next time."

"Yeah, I guess."

Mom closed the car door and spoke to Mrs. Jordan through the open window. "Tonight's a Hopkinsville night for you, isn't it?"

"Yes. Tom and I really enjoy visiting with those folks. It's nice to do something that makes other people feel good and makes you feel good at the same time."

"Well, *I* don't feel good about it," Kendra said from the back seat. "My foot hurts."

"Unhappy camper?" Mom said.

Mrs. Jordan nodded. "She's at that awkward stage. Too old for us to drag her along when she doesn't want to go, but too young to stay by herself when we're so far away."

"Steve and I would be happy to have her go with us tonight. We're meeting his grandparents for pizza."

"I hate to impose on your family time," Mrs. Jordan said.

"It's no imposition. Grampa and Gramma enjoy having Kendra around."

Kendra's mom turned halfway around in her seat. "Would that be all right with you, Miss Priss? Does your foot hurt too much to have some pizza?"

❦ ⊱⊰ ❦

The pizza place in Cadiz isn't one of the chains. It's just a local restaurant that serves lasagna and spaghetti along with pizza. My grandmother doesn't like pizza. She always gets spaghetti with some kind of white sauce on it. Alfred's sauce, I think they call it. I don't know who Alfred is, but his sauce looks kind of icky, like watered-down glue. To me, spaghetti just doesn't look right unless it's got red sauce on it.

The place was so busy we had to wait outside for a table. Through the window I saw Doc walk up to the cashier's counter and pay for his meal. He spotted us as he came out the door.

"Well, hello," he said.

Mom introduced him to my grandparents. They talked for a minute, then Doc turned to Kendra and me.

"That was an intriguing note on my windshield this afternoon. How did you find out about Amanda being a blonde?"

"There's a book about the history of our church," Kendra said. "Look at page 32."

"The church probably has one," I said. "Ask Mrs. Palmer to show it to you the next time you see her."

"I'll certainly do that." Doc looked back at the door. There came Mrs. Palmer. She must have been in the restroom. She stopped beside him, slipped her arm through his, and said hello to everybody.

"We'd better be going," Doc said. "We're browsing the antique malls this evening. Enjoy your supper."

Kendra and I watched them head off down the street. Some of the old stores in downtown Cadiz have gone out of business and been turned into antique stores. Some more places have gone out of business since the bypass was opened a few years ago and Wal-Mart and Home Depot started building out there.

"They look like my cousin and her boyfriend," Kendra said.

"Why does Doc want to go out with *her*?" I muttered.

"Maybe because he likes her," my mom said. I didn't realize she'd heard me. "And maybe because they're both lonely."

"But old people don't go on dates, do they?" Kendra said.

"'Old'?" My grampa rumbled like the giant in 'Jack and the Beanstalk.' "What do you mean 'old'?"

"Doc's fifty-five," Kendra said, drawing closer to me.

"I'm fifty-nine," Grampa said. "And I don't think of myself as old."

"But you're not dating anybody," Kendra said.

"He'd better not be." Gramma elbowed him in the ribs. My mom laughed.

"You have to understand, Kendra," Mom said, "just because people are a little older and a husband or wife has died, that doesn't mean they can't begin new friendships."

"But don't they still love the people they were married to?"

"I'm sure they do. But they're sad and lonely. Meeting somebody new that they like can ease their pain."

"It looks like Doc and Mrs. Palmer like each other a lot," I said.

We watched as Mrs. Palmer laughed at something Doc said. They stopped in front of a store window, but they didn't look like they were paying attention to anything in it. Mrs. Palmer was looking up at Doc, and he couldn't seem to take his eyes off her.

"It's nice to see young people enjoying themselves," Grampa said. "Leona's had a rough time since Fred died."

Somebody ahead of us got a table, so we moved into the restaurant. We were next. I decided to ask a question I had thought about a lot, but never had the nerve to ask.

"Uh, Mom ... ?" Maybe I wouldn't ask.

"Yes, dear?"

Shoot, if I didn't ask now, I'd probably never get the chance. "Would you ... would you ever ... marry somebody else?"

I could tell from the way Mom and my grandparents looked at one another that nobody had seen *that* question coming. I started thinking about it in fifth grade when my friend Derrick's mother got remarried. He really didn't like his stepfather. Then, just before we started sixth grade, Derrick had to move because his stepfather got a job in Louisville.

Mom took a long time to answer. That scared me. Finally she said, "Well, hon, when you lose somebody you love—however it happens—you think for a while that you'll never be able to love anybody else as much. But in time you realize you have to open yourself up to other possibilities. The worst thing you can do when you lose someone is to shut off your feelings."

She wasn't answering my question directly. That *really* scared me. "But would you ever marry somebody else?"

"I haven't met another man I want to marry. Maybe I will someday. Meanwhile, we're getting along okay, aren't we?" She gave me a hug.

"Yeah, we're doing fine." Most days I believed it.

The owner of the restaurant came up to us with a handful of menus. "We've got a table for you. Just follow me."

Kendra was the only one who needed the menu. My family came here often enough that we all knew what we wanted. After we gave the waitress our orders I wondered what we would talk about. I didn't want to talk any more about my mom marrying somebody else. She looked like she was trying not to cry.

"So," Grampa said, "Professor Crisp is helping you two find out something about that old grave, I hear."

"He helped us find some old records in the church." For once I didn't mind talking about Kendra's 'case.' Mom seemed glad to have something else to talk about, too.

"What have you learned so far?"

"A little girl named Amanda Allen is buried there," Kendra said. "She died when she was six. Her father was pastor of the church when the Civil War started. He was forced to resign in the summer of 1862."

"All of that was in the church records?"

"Yes, sir. And today we went to the Historical Society and looked at some old newspapers. We found out where Reverend Allen came from, and he was against slavery, and against the war."

"He was against *all* war," I said.

"He must have been a brave man to think that way with a war going on all around him," Mom said.

"We think he might have helped slaves escape, too," Kendra said, "on the Underground Railroad."

"Why do you think that?" Grampa asked.

"Because of some stuff we read in those newspapers. We want to go back to the cemetery and look around some more."

You want to go back, I thought.

"What do you expect to find?" Mom asked.

"Maybe where the Allens' house was."

"Why would their house be in the cemetery?" Grampa asked.

"Amanda wasn't buried in the cemetery," I said. "The deacons wouldn't let the Allens bury her there. Where she's buried wasn't part of the cemetery then. And we know the Allens bought a farm on Williams Road."

"That's some impressive detective work," Grampa said.

The waitress brought our order. Gramma had her spaghetti with Alfred's sauce and the rest of us shared breadsticks and a super-large pizza with everything, except no olives on one half. Kendra and I both hate olives.

Before she took her first bite Kendra leaned over to me and whispered, "Ask your grandmother about Ezra Clay."

"Do you want to ruin our supper?"

"You said you would ask her the next time you saw her."

By now I should have learned that, if I tell Kendra I'm going to do something, she'll make sure I do it. I finished one bite of pizza.

"Gramma," I said, "there was this one deacon who was really mean to the Allens. His name was Ezra Clay. Is that anybody in our family?"

Gramma put her fork down. Her face looked funny, like her Alfred's sauce didn't taste right. "I'd ... I'd have to check my father's Bible," she said slowly.

"Could we do that after supper?" Kendra asked. "It could be really important."

When Gramma didn't answer, Grampa said, "Sure. We can also look through that box of old pictures in the drawer of our dresser. Who knows what we might find?"

CHAPTER 15

WHEN WE GOT to Gramma and Grampa's house Grampa took Mom into the kitchen. That usually meant he wanted to talk to her about my dad. They had probably gotten a letter or a phone call from him. I guess I ought to be interested, but my dad hasn't shown much interest in me the last few years, so why should I care? I followed Gramma and Kendra to the other end of the house.

The Clay family Bible sat on the mahogany dresser in Gramma and Grampa's bedroom. Gramma took it down and set it on a small desk in a corner of the room. She sat in the chair, and Kendra and I stood on either side of her. The Bible looked really old. Most of the gold lettering had worn off and when you touched the cover it left spots on your fingers, like pollen from a flower.

"A long time ago," Gramma said, "Bibles had a page in them for people to record their family's births, deaths, weddings, that sort of thing. If something was written in a Bible, it was considered as reliable as an official document."

She turned to a page between the Old and New Testaments. It had a border of vines and leaves around it. Across the top of the page fancy letters said 'Family Tree.'

"As you can see," Gramma said, "different people wrote things in here over the years. The handwritings and the inks change from time to time."

Most of the handwriting was fancy, kind of spidery.

"That's like the handwriting we saw in the church ledgers," Kendra said.

"That's the way people were taught to write back in the 1800s," Gramma said. "It takes longer, but nobody was in such a hurry in those days. Now, Ezekiel Clay was the original owner of the Bible." She pointed to his name. "He recorded the names of his parents and grandparents, and of his two brothers and three sisters. The rest of the chart follows his own family. He was married in 1827. He and his wife had several children, but only Ezra and his sister Hannah lived past the age of two. Ezra was born in 1830 and married in 1850."

"That handwriting is different from the first handwriting," Kendra said.

"That's right," Gramma said. "Ezekiel Clay died in 1841, as you see here. I think his wife entered some of this information until Ezra was old enough to take over as head of the family."

"Gosh," I said, "Ezra was only eleven when his dad died."

"It wasn't unusual in those days for young children to lose their parents," Gramma said. "They had to grow up fast."

I leaned over Gramma's shoulder to see the list of names and dates. "There's his son Jonathan. He died from the flu. Ezra had two other children, it says. They were younger than Jonathan."

"And, look," Kendra said, "Ezra died on December 4, 1862. My gosh, he was only thirty-two."

"Was he killed in the Civil War?" I asked.

"No, he wasn't," Gramma said. I expected her to say more. Usually it just takes one question to get her started and she'll tell you the life history of just about anybody in the county.

"What happened to him?"

There was a long pause before Gramma said, "He hanged himself, on the tree next to that little girl's grave."

"Why?" Kendra and I asked.

"Nobody ever knew. My grandmother suspected he had done something he was ashamed of, but nobody in the family talked about it. If what you've found out about Reverend Allen and his house being burned is true, you may have found the answer. I told you, you might learn more than we wanted to know."

"Don't you think it's important to learn the truth, Gramma, whatever it may be?"

"Some truths can be painful, Steve. But, since you've come this far, you might as well hear the rest of the story. I've had a few bits of it all along, like old pieces from a jigsaw puzzle that you keep in a box, just in case you find the puzzle they're missing from. When I heard what you said tonight at supper, I realized these pieces might fit into your puzzle."

She got up and went back to the dresser. Opening the

bottom drawer, she pulled out a box. If you find this kind of box under the Christmas tree, you know you're getting clothes. She set it on the bed and took the lid off. Kendra and I saw dozens of old photographs loose in the box, and envelopes that must have held more pictures. There were also two small notebooks in plastic bags. Gramma took them out and brought them over to the desk.

"This is Jacob Clay's diary," she said. "He was Ezra's youngest child. He was only three when his father died. And this ... this is Ezra Clay's diary."

Kendra and I gasped.

"It won't tell you very much," Gramma said. "It's been years since I looked at it. The handwriting's awfully hard to read. I don't recall seeing anything about Reverend Allen. It talks mostly about Ezra's family and things he did from day to day on his farm. The weather must have been important to him as a farmer. He spent about half of each entry describing it."

The little book's cover was badly scratched. As she opened it a couple of pages fell loose from the binding.

"It was a cheap book to begin with," Gramma said, "and it hasn't always been treated very kindly. My grandmother used it as a doorstop. That's where I first noticed it."

"A doorstop!" Kendra said. "Why do people abuse valuable old things like that?"

"They don't always realize they're valuable," Gramma said. "One generation's trash is the next generation's treasure. Like those old baseball cards of my son's that I almost threw out. Steve would never have forgiven me, would you?"

She turned the pages of the diary carefully. Once in a while she would stop to read something to us. On one page Ezra described lying in bed at night listening to rats "larger than a cat" scampering over the floor of his house.

Kendra shuddered. "Gross! I can't *stand* rats."

The next morning Ezra and his wife discovered that their baby girl, Sarah, had been bitten twice during the night but "seemed to be suffering no ill effects." A few days later, March 3, 1862, he reported it "was snowing at daybrake."

But around noon ...

it commensed raining and has continued to rain up to this time (6 ½ PM) and is raining faster at this time than at any other time today.

We had a hard time last night with Sarah. Never went to sleep until after Eleven. Then was up with her agin a little after One O'clock.

Startid and went to Freemans and Bakers this morn to try to sell our Hog or any thing I had to get some money to buy some thing to eat, but did not succeede in selling any thing.

"Those poor people!" Kendra said. "Is it all like that?"

Gramma nodded. "Most of it is. They lived a hard life."

Something didn't add up for me. "If they were so poor, what did they do with their slaves? How did they feed them?"

"Oh, they didn't have any slaves. Ezekiel, his father, had owned four, but after he died the family had to sell them to pay off some debts."

"But if Ezra didn't own any slaves, why would he have been for the Confederates in the Civil War?"

"I don't know, hon. Slavery wasn't the only reason the war was fought. Ezra never says why he was on that side."

"I'll bet Doc would love to see this," I said. "It sure is hard to read, though. His handwriting's worse than mine."

"His spelling wasn't so good, either," Kendra said. As sixth-grade spelling bee champ, she would notice that sort of thing.

I had to defend my ancestor. "He spells words like they sound. 'Started' sounds like it ought to rhyme with 'did.' It's not his fault. The problem is with the crazy English language."

"I'd be happy to let Professor Crisp look at this," Gramma said. "Now I want to show you the end of it. Ezra and a man named John Hardaway were planning something that involved Hardaway's taking information to friends of his in Tennessee."

"Information about what?" Kendra asked.

"He never says exactly," Gramma replied. "I think it had to do with slaves. He quotes the verse where Paul says slaves should be obedient to their masters." She turned a couple of pages. "Yes, here it is. 'That is the New Covenant,' he says, 'which was given in place of the Old, no matter what some may think'."

"I'll bet he had read Reverend Allen's letter in the paper," I said. "What's the date of that entry, Gramma?"

"August 11, 1862."

"That fits exactly," Kendra said. "The letter was published on the seventh, and the deacons made him resign on the fourteenth. What does it say next?"

"He didn't write every day in the late summer and early fall. I guess he was busy harvesting whatever they managed to grow that summer. By the middle of October he was writing almost every day again. The death of his son, Jonathan, hit him really hard. He quotes another Bible verse: 'Would that I had died instead of you'."

"About a dozen people in the church died from the flu in October," I said.

"Oh, my," Gramma said. "How dreadful."

"Does he say any more about what he and this man Hardaway were going to do?" Kendra asked.

"They decided somebody had to do something about 'the situation.' That's all he calls it. Hardaway will tell some people in Tennessee about it and let them 'deal with it in whatever way they deem most appropriate.' He wrote that on October 25, 1862."

"That's about ten days before Confederate soldiers raided here and burned the Allens' house," Kendra said.

"Was anyone killed?" Gramma asked.

"We think so," I said, "but we don't have any proof."

"I don't know if this proves anything," Gramma said, "but on November 8 he writes:

> *My God, what have I done? Hardaway said they wouldn't hurt nobody. Just scare them, maybe run them out of Kentucky. If I had knowed our efforts to deal with the situation would end like this, I would never have got involved. I sware it! I am no better than Judas. That's what he called me, and that's who I am.*

Mom poked her head in at the door. Her eyes were red and puffy and she was carrying a wad of tissues. "Are you finding out anything?" she asked. She was trying not to sound like she'd been crying.

"It's incredible!" Kendra said. "Ezra Clay was the one who told the Confederates that the Allens were hiding runaway slaves. Then he was sorry for what he'd done."

Gramma carefully turned a couple of pages in the diary. "He writes about how depressed he is several times in November. He says he tried to give the money back to Hardaway: 'I throwed it at his feet when he refused to taik it. Can I be any more like Judas?'"

She stopped and peered at us over the top of her reading glasses. "I guess the soldiers gave them a reward."

"The situations are certainly similar," Grampa said. "Judas got money for showing the priests where Jesus was so they could arrest him. When he tried to give it back, the priests wouldn't take it, so he threw it at them."

"Yeah," Kendra said quietly. "Then he went out and hanged himself."

"The last entry in the diary is dated December 3, 1862," Gramma said. "It starts with a quotation from the twenty-seventh chapter of Matthew:

> 'Then Judas, which had _betrayed_ him, when he
> saw that he was condemned, _repented_ himself,
> and brought again the thirty pieces of silver to the
> chief priests and elders, saying, I have sinned in
> that I have betrayed the innocent blood. And they
> said, What is that to us? See thou to that. And he
> cast down the pieces of silver in the temple, and
> departed, and went and _hanged_ himself.'

"Those three words are underlined," Gramma said. "'Betrayed,' 'repented,' and 'hanged.' Then, at the bottom of the page, he wrote:

> I am like Judas in all else. Why do I hesitate to
> follow him in this final step? What else could he
> have done? What else can I do?

We were all quiet, like at the end of a prayer. Then Mom blew her nose and said, "The men in this family don't do things halfway, do they? When they decide to take action, they take _serious_ action." I didn't think she was trying to be funny.

"There's some bitter truth to that," Gramma said. She looked Mom right in the eye. I could tell they knew something they weren't telling me. "They don't always consider the effect their actions will have on those around them, either. Ezra left a widow with two young children. She had to go live with her in-laws. She never remarried. They barely scraped through. Jacob, Ezra's son, says in his diary that, from his earliest memories of his mother, she was a tired, bitter woman."

Mom sniffed and wiped her nose. "A woman doesn't have to react that way to negative events. She can focus on the positive things in her life." She hugged me tightly. Whatever news she'd gotten from Atlanta, it must have been pretty bad.

Kendra sat on the bed beside the box of pictures, with one leg tucked under her and the other dangling over the edge of the bed. Her bandaged ankle bulged over her sneaker. "Can we look at some of the pictures? Do you know who the people are?"

"Only the more recent ones, I'm afraid," Gramma said. "Any from before my mother's generation weren't labeled very carefully, if at all."

"If we had that church picture with us," I said, "we could compare some of these pictures with that. The man in that picture who looks like one of these men should be Ezra Clay."

"If Ezra showed up for the picture," Kendra said. "And it might be hard to tell anyway. All you white people look alike." She smiled and we all laughed.

"All these men have beards and dark suits," Gramma said. "I'm not sure I could tell them apart."

"A magnifying glass would help," Grampa said. "We ought to have one handy the next time we get this box out."

"I guess it is getting kind of late," Kendra said, checking her watch. "My mom and dad ought to be home in a few minutes."

I shuffled through a few more pictures. "Can't we look just a little longer? There might be something important in here."

"Now who's getting carried away?" Kendra said.

"Well, we know what Amanda and her family looked like. Don't you want to know about the other people in the case, too?"

"You just called it a 'case'," Kendra gloated. "And I have witnesses. Sounds to me like you're getting interested in this dumb mystery stuff."

"Well, a lot of things are starting to fit together. Like when you just need a couple of more baseball cards to have a complete set. And the sooner we get this figured out, the sooner I can practice my pitching."

"Yeah, yeah," Kendra said. She picked up a picture and studied it, then showed it to Gramma. "Do you know who this is?"

"I'm afraid not, dear. It looks like it was made in the 1890's or so, to judge by the style of the clothes."

I looked over Gramma's shoulder at the picture. It showed a woman and a man with a beard standing in front of a small house. The house looked as old and poor as the people.

"Does that remind you of anything, Steve?" Kendra asked.

"How could it? I've never seen this picture before."

"Take a closer look. Focus on their feet."

I looked at the picture again. Mom, Gramma, and Grampa all studied it, too.

"What should we be looking for?" Mom asked.

Kendra just smiled and started singing an old hymn, "On Christ the solid *rock* I stand."

I looked hard at the picture again. I wanted to figure out what she was hinting at, just to stop her from singing. Then it hit me. "Okay, I get it."

"You do?" Mom said. "How?"

"Tuesday, right?" I said to Kendra. "When you tripped on your crutches?"

"Right *on*!" She held up her hand for a high five.

"What are you two talking about?" Grampa asked.

"You had to be there," I said.

"Let's go back tomorrow morning," Kendra said.

"If you think you're on to something," Mom said, "shouldn't you tell Professor Crisp? He'll know what you need to do next."

"We'll have to pry him away from Mrs. Palmer," I said.

CHAPTER 16

"HERE IT IS," Kendra said. "Where Doc started scraping some of the dirt off."

I watched as she poked the tip of her shovel into the ground beside the big stone she had fallen over a couple of days ago. The morning was already too warm to be using the shovel, broom and small potting spade we had brought from my garage when we set out for Amanda's grave.

"Okay, let's see what we've got." She punched the shovel into the ground.

"You aren't planning to dig it up, are you? Doc said we shouldn't mess with it."

"I'm just going to dig around it, to see how big it is."

"Do you really think it was a doorstep?"

Kendra's face brightened. "Not just any doorstep. The Allens' doorstep. You want to give me a hand? This is hard to do with my bad ankle."

I took the shovel. She straightened up and pushed her hair out of her face, rubbing a streak of dirt across her forehead.

It took me only a few minutes to strip away the thin layer of dirt that covered the large slab of stone. Then I swept it off with the broom, and we stepped back to study it.

What we had uncovered was a single piece of stone about four feet long, two feet from front to back and six inches from top to bottom. With the dirt cleared away from it, we could see the wear on one edge where people's feet had scuffed it for years.

"Amanda actually climbed up that step," Kendra said. She sounded like she was looking at something Babe Ruth or Mickey Mantle had touched. But, I had to admit to myself, I felt kind of funny, too. This was something the Allens actually used. When I stood on it, I felt like I was connected to them.

"I wonder if she sat on that step to rest," I said.

"She must have," Kendra said. She sat on the stone, drawing her knees up and clutching them to her. I sat beside her.

"I wonder what she saw when she sat here," Kendra said.

"The road was here, at least a dirt road. And the church was at the top of the hill. And we know there were graves here already."

"The other side of the road must have looked really different, though," Kendra said. "More trees, no houses or cottages, and no view of the lake through that gap in the trees over there. No lake to have a view of."

Neither of us said anything for a minute.

"Doc's car isn't in front of his cottage, is it?" Kendra said.

"I guess he's out doing more stuff about selling his house. We've got a lot to tell him."

"There's one more thing we need to find out about, though," Kendra said. "If this is the Allens' house, it was burned. I wonder if we can find any trace of the fire."

"Could you do that after this long?"

"I don't know. But if this is the door step, the house would have been right behind us." She stood up and picked up the shovel. "Let's see if we can find anything."

We scraped around behind the doorstep with the shovel and the spade for a few minutes until we hit something solid. It made a thunk, like wood, not a clank, like stone.

"Is that a log?" I said.

"Oh, my gosh! Part of it is black." Kendra dropped to her knees and touched the top of the log. Her hand came away sooty, like she had rubbed it on piece of charcoal. "Steve, this was burned!"

"I don't think we ought to dig any more," I said. "We could mess up something important if we poke around by ourselves."

"I guess you're right," Kendra said, but she wasn't happy about it. "At least we know what happened to the Allens. They must have died in the fire."

"We can't prove that."

"But we found their house."

"This was *a* house and it looks like it was burned. We haven't found a mailbox with the Allens' name on it."

"No, but if it's not the Allens' house, why is Amanda buried over there?" Kendra pointed toward the tombstone.

"Yeah, that's pretty strong evidence. I don't think it could be anybody else's house."

"And it was burned, like the house in the newspaper article." She rubbed her hand on the charred wood again.

"But that doesn't mean the Allens died here."

"What else could have happened to them?"

"Almost anything. We just don't have any proof. Isn't that what detectives are supposed to find? Proof?"

"Okay. You've got me. We haven't found a mailbox with their name on it, or anything that definite. But we might if we keep digging. We might even find their bodies."

I grabbed the shovel before she could stick it in the ground again. "Do you really want to do that by ourselves? I think my mom was right. It's time to talk to Doc and let him help us before we mess something up. There are probably rules about how you dig up a historical place like this. Doc would know."

She tried to take the shovel from me, but I didn't let go.

"All right," she said. "It's just frustrating. We know what Amanda and her parents looked like. We know why her father was forced to resign. We know they were helping slaves escape. We're standing *in* their house. We know it was burned. But there's so much more we *don't* know."

Before we started back up the hill we stood in front of Amanda's grave for a minute. Kendra rubbed her eyes and sniffed. I didn't feel like crying, but I patted Kendra on the shoulder to let her know I understood how she felt.

As we turned away from the grave, I tucked the spade in my other back pocket, the one that didn't have my notebook in it, and took the broom from Kendra. She used the shovel as a crutch.

"Do you have more doughnuts at your house?" she asked.

"There were three or four left after breakfast."

"Good. I could use a doughnut. And some juice."

"I'm just thirsty. It's hot today."

I was practicing my swing with the broom, like it was a baseball bat. I put down a perfect bunt and dropped the broom. When I reached down to pick it up my head was turned toward the old barn in the vacant field behind the cemetery. What I saw there made me drop to the ground and pull Kendra down with me behind the hedge.

"What's the big deal?" she said.

"Ssh! Look." I pointed through the bushes at the old barn.

"It's Dwayne," Kendra said.

Dwayne was approaching the rickety old building from the other direction, pushing his bike and looking around constantly to see if anyone had noticed him.

"I wonder what he's up to," Kendra muttered.

"Nothing good, I bet."

"Let's go see." She started to push through the hedge.

I didn't budge. "This is as close as I want to get to Dwayne."

"He won't see us. We can peek through some of the cracks in the side of the barn. There are two of us. He wouldn't dare try anything against us. Come on!"

Without waiting for my answer she pushed through the hedge and started across the field, crouching down in the tall weeds. I sighed and my shoulders sagged as I set off after her. I thought about carrying the shovel with me for protection but decided I couldn't be very sneaky carrying something that big.

Kendra and I had been in the old barn a few times, in spite of our parents' warnings, but it wasn't somewhere we liked to hang out. Anything interesting had been removed years ago. The ladder up to the loft was so rotten we were afraid to climb it. Every time the wind blew, the whole building seemed to sway and groan. Just standing near enough to it to peek through one of the cracks where the siding boards had warped and separated made me nervous. I put my hands on the boards like I could hold them up.

At first I didn't see anything but an empty barn, plenty of spider webs, a broken plow handle, and other junk.

"Where did he go?" Kendra whispered.

I stood back from the barn and glanced around, suddenly afraid that Dwayne was going to sneak up on us.

"Oh, my gosh! Steve, look!"

Kendra grabbed my arm and almost threw me up against the barn. With my face mushed against the boards I had no choice but to look. What I saw was like a scene out of a movie. A grain storage bin on the other side of the barn was moving to one side.

By itself!

CHAPTER 17

I WATCH SPOOKY movies, but I don't believe in ghosts or anything like that. I don't believe that wooden boxes can move by themselves. I knew something or somebody had to be moving that storage bin. Kendra and I had played in it. It was heavy.

Then Dwayne's head appeared, coming out of a hole under the bin. He climbed all the way out of the hole and dusted himself off. If he had been facing us, he might have noticed our eyeballs practically bulging through the cracks. But he didn't seem to know we were watching him. He pulled the bin over the hole. Then he kicked some dirt and straw around it until you couldn't tell anything had been moved.

"Why didn't we see that when we were in there?" Kendra said, almost too loudly.

"Ssh!" I slapped her arm and she slapped me back.

Dwayne left the barn. I peeked around the corner and saw him riding away on his bike. When he was out of sight around a curve I motioned for Kendra to follow me.

The barn had two doors that opened outward. One was hanging so low it was stuck in the ground. The other hung on one hinge. Kendra started to pull it back.

"Don't!" I said. "It looks like it'll fall off. And we don't want Dwayne to be able to tell anybody's been here."

I was starting to squeeze in between the doors when Kendra said, "Wait a minute. Look at this." She pointed to some designs scratched into the door frame.

I came back out and stood beside her. "Yeah, we saw those when we were here before. Remember? There's a cow, a rooster, a plow, and some other stuff."

Kendra put her finger on one of the designs. "But this one's a drinking gourd."

I put my face up to the design. It was so faint you wouldn't notice it unless you were looking for it. "Just like the one on Amanda's grave."

"Do you know what that means?" Kendra asked.

"No. What?"

"It's elementary, my dear Patterson," she said in that fakey British accent.

"Don't do that, Kendra. Just tell me what it means."

She talked to me over her shoulder as she squeezed between the barn doors. "It means Dwayne has found the slaves' hiding place, the Allens' station on the Underground Railroad."

∽❦ᘓ❦ᘐ❦∾

The light in the barn was dim, and the place still smelled like animals had been in it until a few days ago. I wouldn't have been surprised if I stepped in a pile of something. We walked over to the grain storage bin that Dwayne had moved. When we slid it back we saw a deep hole, like a mine shaft. It was about three feet on each side. The light was so dim I couldn't tell how deep it was. The top of a metal ladder was visible.

"Hey, that's our ladder," Kendra said. "See? 'Jordan,' right on the top rung. Somebody stole it out of our garage last fall."

"At least we know it won't break on us," I said. "Who's going down there?"

Kendra touched her ankle. "My foot's bothering me. I guess I've been walking on it too much. I don't know about going down a ladder ..."

"Okay," I said. "You keep an eye out for Dwayne." I took a deep breath, lay on my stomach, and found the top rung of the ladder with my feet. I wanted to get down and up as quick as I could. Dwayne could come back at any minute, and I didn't think the fact that we outnumbered him would make any difference.

When I got to the bottom of the ladder I could hardly see anything. The dim light in the barn didn't reach that far down. By feeling around I realized there was no wall on one side of the shaft. I leaned forward and moved my arms into the opening on that side, but I couldn't tell how far it went. The opening was high enough for me to stand up in. Anybody taller than me would have to stoop. I didn't want to go any farther without some light. I wished I had one of those miner's hats with a light on top of it.

"What do you see?" Kendra called down. When I looked up her head was framed in the opening of the shaft, like a picture. The light behind her made her look kind of like an angel.

"I can't see much of anything. It's really dark down here." As my eyes adjusted to the darkness I stumbled over a big plastic storage box with a lid on it, just inside the opening. "Didn't somebody steal a plastic container out of your garage too?"

"Is there one down there? How big is it?"

"It's about three feet long and half as wide."

"That sound likes it. Somebody emptied the stuff my mom was storing in it. Is there anything in that one?"

I opened the box and felt around inside it. My hand landed on something metal and glass. I picked it up and held it close to my face. "Hey, this is that camping lantern that was stolen out of our garage."

"Do the batteries still work?"

Kendra and I had used the lantern when we made a tent out of blankets spread over Mom's dining room table. I felt around until I found the switch. When the beam of light clicked on I felt better. I'm not usually afraid of tight places or of the dark, but a tight place in the dark ... that's creepy.

"Way to go!" Kendra said. "Now what do you see?"

"Don't talk so loud! Everything echoes in here." I held the lantern up so the light shined toward her. "Are you watching for Dwayne at all? He'll stomp both of us if he catches us here."

"Then the sooner you look around, the sooner we can leave. That lantern's not giving much light. The batteries must be low."

I held the lantern in front of me so I could see into the opening. "It's kind of a tunnel, but it only goes about ten feet. Then there's a wall."

"What's in the plastic box?"

"A bunch of comic books, in those plastic bags like Mr. Morse uses. And a couple of candy bars and three cans of root beer." The W*onder Woman* comic I had paid for was on top.

"I want to take a look," Kendra said.

"There's nothing else down here," I told her, but before I could say anything else she had climbed down the ladder and was standing next to me.

"I'm glad your foot healed up so quickly," I said.

She took the lantern from me and shined it around the tunnel. "Reverend Allen was a coal miner before he became a minister. I'll bet he dug this."

"I guess he didn't have time to finish it, though."

She had to duck her head to get into the tunnel. As if I needed another reminder that she was taller than me.

"I wish you waited for me to go up before you came down here," I said as I followed her into the tunnel. "Dwayne could come back without us knowing it."

"Relax, will you? He's long gone." She opened the plastic box. "Boy, he sure has been stealing a lot of comics, hasn't he?"

"I'm going up and keep a lookout for him," I said.

"It's too late for that, Steverino," a distant voice echoed.

We rushed back to the opening of the shaft in time to see the ladder rising out of our reach. When it was gone, Dwayne leaned over the opening of the shaft, his face twisted with rage.

"That's what you get for messin' in my stuff!"

"*Your* stuff? You stole it," Kendra said.

"And you're gonna snitch on me, aren't you? Just like you did in the bookstore!"

"I gave you the money to pay for the comic. Mr. Morse didn't do anything to you."

"But he'll be watchin' me every time I go in there now. I won't be able to get any more. Unless you're gonna buy 'em for me."

Kendra shook her fist at him. "Why don't you try buying them yourself, you ... ?" My elbow in her ribs cut her short.

"What—what are you going to do to us?" I asked, unable to control a shiver in my voice.

"I'm not gonna do anything to you," Dwayne said. "I'll just pull the grain bin back over this openin' and walk away."

"You can't leave us here!" Kendra yelled.

"Oh, I'll come back, maybe by ..." he looked at his watch "... tomorrow. Monday at the latest."

"Dwayne, you're crazy," Kendra said. "People will be looking for us." She stretched out her arms like she could reach him and stop him.

"Yeah. You're real popular, ain't you? If I disappeared for a few days, nobody'd notice. I bet if you're ten minutes late gettin' home, they call the cops to find their precious Kendra and Steve."

He put his hand on the grain bin and started to pull. A fine shower of dirt rained down on us.

"Come on, Dwayne," I said. "Think about what you're doing. If something happens to us, you'll be in a whole lot more trouble than you would be just for shoplifting. We won't tell anybody about this stuff or this place."

"You're just sayin' that so I'll let you out," Dwayne said.

"Somebody will find us." I wished I was as sure of that as I was trying to sound.

"I don't think so," Dwayne said. "This place is pretty hard to find."

"We found it," Kendra shot back. "So did you. Somebody else will find it."

"Not likely. I only found it 'cause I saw a chipmunk run down a hole. A pretty big hole, it turned out. You saw me comin' out of the hole, I guess. But nobody's gonna see you, 'cause you won't be comin' out 'til I say so."

"Dwayne, please don't!" I yelled.

The light began to disappear as Dwayne pulled the grain bin over the opening of the shaft. There was only a small square of light left. "Nice talkin' to you," he said, "but my dad and I are goin' fishin' in a little while. Oh, by the way. The batteries in that light are gettin' low. I just went to get some new ones."

"Come on, Dwayne!" I said. "Don't leave us here in the dark."

"Oh, poor Steverino. Do you still sleep with a night light? Tell you what, to show you I'm really a nice guy ..." His hand appeared in the hole, clutching a package of batteries.

"Where did you steal them from?" Kendra said.

Dwayne's hand pulled back and he stuck his head into the small hole and sneered at us. "You've always gotta make some smart crack, don't you? Just for that, no batteries."

"If you leave us down here," Kendra cried, "we'll tear up every one of these comics!"

I clamped my hand over her mouth and whispered. "Shut up, will you?"

Dwayne hesitated, then said, "You do anything to those comics, I'll come back and pound you good. Both of you."

The grain bin settled into place with a thud.

CHAPTER 18

"**STEVE! WHAT DO** we do now?" Kendra clawed at the wall of the shaft like she wanted to climb straight up it.

"We could read some comics." I tried to sound calmer than I felt. One of us needed to be calm. "Our folks will start looking for us when we don't show up for lunch. When we hear them calling, we'll yell back and they'll find us."

I hoped it would be that easy. Since we had been told not to play in the barn and since our parents knew that we never played in the barn, it would probably be one of the last places anybody would look. Even if they did look here, they wouldn't know about the grain bin. Would we hear anybody looking for us up there? Would they hear us calling from down here?

"There probably won't be anybody home at lunch time," Kendra reminded me. "Our mothers went to that rummage sale in Cadiz, and they'll stop somewhere for lunch. My dad's building bookshelves in the basement. When he's doing something like that he forgets about everything else. We could be down here for a while. And pretty soon we're going to be in the dark."

"And whose fault is that?"

"I'm sorry. Okay? I know I shouldn't have said what I did. I'm used to talking to the big jerk that way. Do you think he'll really leave us down here for a couple of days?"

"I don't know what he might do. But Dwayne isn't our problem right now. We need to think of some way out of here."

"Like that's going to happen," Kendra said, arching her head back to stare up the shaft.

"It won't happen if we don't try. We can't just sit here."

"You're right, Steve. Sorry. I'm scared. Aren't you?"

"Not really," I lied. "There's nothing down here to hurt us. It's just a matter of figuring out how we're going to get out."

My little pep talk seemed to help her more than it did me. I felt like we were trapped and were going to stay trapped until Dwayne came back. And I was scared. My stomach felt even worse than it did when I had to go to the dentist.

"Okay." Kendra looked around. "What do we need to get out of here?"

"A ladder. There's one up there in the barn. But we need a ladder to get to the ladder."

"You're not helping, Steve. We've got to find some other way to reach the bottom of the grain bin."

"How do we do that, Sherlock?"

"Let's do a little math, my dear Patterson. My dad said his twelve-foot ladder was stolen. Standing almost straight the ladder almost reached the top, so this shaft must be at least twelve feet deep. I'm five feet even, and you're four feet eight—"

"Four-foot-nine. I've grown an inch since my birthday."

"Yeah, that'll make all the difference."

"Ha-ha."

"Okay. Five feet plus four feet *nine* inches. That still leaves us with a couple of feet to go."

"More than that. You're figuring like one of us would be standing on the other one's head. But we'll be standing on shoulders. That's where you have to measure from."

"Yeah, I forgot about that." Kendra shined the lantern upward. Two handles were attached to the bottom of the grain bin so somebody could slide it from underneath. "Let's try it anyway. My arms are longer. I'll stand on your shoulders."

She put the lantern on the ground. I stooped down and let her stand on my shoulders. With both of us bracing ourselves against the walls of the shaft, I was able to straighten up.

"Can you reach it?"

"No, I'm still a couple of feet away from it. Even if I could reach it, the bin's heavy. I'll have to be standing on something solid to be able to slide it."

"Rats!" I said.

"Don't worry. We'll find a way out."

"No, I mean I just saw a rat."

"Oh, gross!" Kendra cried. She lost her balance and fell on top of me. "Where is it?"

"I think we scared it away. It probably smelled the candy bars." I snapped the lid back on the plastic container.

Kendra grabbed the lantern and waved it around wildly. "We've got to get out of here, Steve! You know I can't stand rats and mice!" She shuddered.

"Hey, calm down. As long as we've got light and keep moving around, I don't think they'll bother us." Like I really know what a rat would do. But I had to make Kendra feel better. And I couldn't let her know how scared I really was.

"We won't have light for long. We've got to find a way out." She shined the lantern up the shaft, then into the tunnel. "What are we going to do? We're stuck here." Her voice wobbled.

I put my arm around her shoulder. "Don't worry. Our folks will be looking for us soon. Think about what Sherlock Holmes would do in this situation. He's so smart he'd probably—I don't know—build an elevator. This looks like an elevator shaft."

Kendra ran her hand over her eyes and laughed. Then she looked up the shaft. "That's a jolly good idea, my dear Patterson," she said in that stupid British accent.

"Don't start that stuff. What are you talking about? What's a good idea?"

"What you just said. Well, sort of. An elevator raises the floor you're standing on. If we could raise the floor of this shaft by a couple of feet, we could reach the handles on that bin."

"Raise the floor? How are we going to do that?"

"We need something solid to stand on." She looked around.

"All we've got is that plastic container. But it's only about six inches high, and I don't think it would hold our weight."

Kendra put a foot on top of the plastic container and leaned on it. "You're right. That's going to collapse if even one of us tries to stand on it."

"There's nothing else here we can stand on," I said.

Kendra looked back into the tunnel. "I wish we had a shovel."

"What good would that do? We're *in* a hole. My grampa says the first rule of holes is, when you're in one, stop digging."

"Very funny. Remind me to laugh someday. If we had a shovel, we could dig some dirt from over there" —she swung the lantern into the tunnel— "and pack it down over here. We could raise the floor in the shaft so we could reach the grain bin. I guess we could dig with our hands ..."

"Wait!" I reached into my back pocket. "I've got my mom's spade. It's not big, but it would be faster than using our hands."

She actually hugged me. "Oh, Steve! That's wonderful." She picked up the plastic container and dumped the stolen comics. "Let's eat the candy bars so the rats won't smell them."

I've eaten candy bars for lots of reasons, but never that one.

"Let's dig in the back wall of the tunnel," she said. "The dirt feels softer there, and we don't want to risk making the shaft cave in on us."

"Good idea. I guess we'll have to take turns, since we've only got one spade."

"I'll go first. I *really* want to get out of here."

While Kendra dug with the spade, I scraped some dirt up with my hands. When we had the plastic container filled, we dumped the dirt onto the floor of the shaft and packed it down. What looked like a lot of dirt when it was loose in the container turned out not to be much when it was packed down. Even after our third load it didn't look like we'd raised the spot where we were planning to stand by more than a few inches.

"Bummer," Kendra said. "All that digging, and that's all we get?"

"I'm going to have a root beer before I go back to work," I said. "You want one?"

"You know I don't like root beer. Besides, it would just make me need to pee sooner. And there's no bathroom down here."

"No problem. We'll just turn off the lantern."

"No! I couldn't stand this place in the dark—with the rats."

"Then you'd better start digging. These batteries aren't going to last much longer." The lantern was dimmer than it was when I turned it on.

"Hurry up and finish your root beer and help me."

"Okay. I'm thirsty. I told you that." Standing in the dark of the shaft, I sipped the root beer. It was warm, but I was really thirsty. Kendra, with the lantern on the ground beside her, kept up a steady rhythm, first a *thunk* as the spade sank into the red clay soil and then a *plop* as another little pile of dirt landed in the plastic box. I had just finished my drink when I heard her gasp.

"What is it? Another rat?"

"No, it's an opening. This isn't a wall. I dug through it."

I stepped into the tunnel to find Kendra scraping frantically. "Look. This isn't the end of the tunnel. There's more to it. This part must have caved in."

We dug with the spade and our hands until we had an opening we could both look through. Kendra shined the lantern into it. A tunnel ran away from us as far as the dim light would let us see.

"Where do you think it goes?" I asked.

Kendra used her finger to draw a diagram in the dirt. "Here's the barn. Here are the doors. The grain bin over the shaft is here. The tunnel runs away from the shaft this way ... Wow. That goes toward the Allens' house!"

"I wonder if it goes all the way. When we get out of here, we'll have to see if there's another end to it under their house."

"The other end would be easier to find," Kendra said, "if we just follow the tunnel."

"I thought you wanted to get out of here. We'll get out if we keep piling up dirt until we can reach the grain bin."

"But this could take us out, maybe faster than trying to get up the shaft. Come on."

"Look, it caved in here. What if it's blocked farther along?"

"Then we turn around. We won't lose anything. Come on, Steve—who knows what we might find?"

She took the lantern and shined it into the tunnel again. It looked passable as far as I could see, about four feet wide and four feet high.

But I still didn't like the idea. And not just because I don't like being in small, narrow places. "We know somebody's going to come looking for us and we know where we can get out at this end. We don't know what we'll run into up there."

Kendra sighed and looked back at the shaft and the little bit of dirt we had already piled up. I hoped she was thinking about what I'd said. Then her eyes got big and she pointed at something. I turned around and saw two rats. Big ones.

Suddenly the shaft got dark. When I turned back around all I saw was Kendra's feet. She was crawling through the opening. And she took the lantern! I had two choices: sit in the dark with the rats, or follow her.

Talk about a no-brainer.

We moved pretty fast in the tunnel. Kendra was trying to get away from the rats and I was just trying to keep up with her and the lantern. I duck-walked at first, but that got uncomfortable, so I dropped to my knees and crawled, like Kendra was doing ahead of me. The tunnel seemed to slope up slightly. About every ten feet it had wooden beams bracing it.

Kendra rounded a curve, leaving me in the dark.

"Hey, slow down. Don't leave me ..." The rest of my sentence was drowned out by Kendra's scream.

I crawled around the curve as fast as I could. Kendra was sitting back on her heels, her hands over her mouth and her eyes wide. In front of her, by the dim light of the lantern, I saw a human skeleton.

CHAPTER 19

"OH, MY GOD!" was all I could say. My mom doesn't like me to say that, but it just popped out. "Oh, my God!"

The skeleton lay on its back, almost blocking the tunnel. The dress it was wearing was partly rotted away.

"Look at the buttons," Kendra said. Neither of us had moved yet. We were both still on our knees, almost like we were praying. "Those white buttons down the front! That's the dress Mrs. Allen was wearing in the church picture."

In that picture she had looked pretty. Now she was all teeth and eyeholes. A spider was crawling out of the left one. I took the lantern from Kendra and swung it around. The dim light fell on two more skeletons a little farther up the tunnel.

"Oh, my gosh!" I said. "I think that one's a man. He's wearing pants."

"And he's got a handcuff thing and broken chain around his wrist," Kendra said, "so I guess he's a runaway slave."

"Come on, let's go back," I said.

"Go back? Why?"

"Who knows how many other skeletons are up there? I don't want to be crawling over them."

"Don't you get it? We must be close to the Allens' house. This is where the slaves hid until they could get to the barn and escape. There has to be a way out—a trap door or something. Let's go!"

She grabbed the lantern from me and stepped over Mrs. Allen. I reached out for the lantern, lost my balance, and fell—right on Mrs. Allen! Her bones rattled, and I could feel them pressing against my chest, like I was lying on a bag of baseball bats.

I couldn't help myself. I screamed.

Kendra came back to me. "Are you all right?" She held out her hand and helped me crawl over Mrs. Allen.

"No, I'm not!" I accidentally kicked some of the bones as I
leaned against the wall of the tunnel, breathing as hard as if I'd
been running out a triple. I brushed my shirt off, but I couldn't
get rid of that feeling of bones pressing against me. "I want to go
back. I've got to get out of this damn tunnel so I can stand up."

"You don't have to talk ugly. Just come right over here."
She led me a few feet farther to where the tunnel widened into a
kind of room with a higher ceiling.

When I could stand up straight I felt like I could breathe
again and I started to calm down. "What is this place?"

"I think it's just under the Allens' house." Kendra shined the
lantern around and we saw bunk beds built into two walls of the
room. On one side a ladder led up to a trap door.

"Look, there are more bodies over there." Kendra pointed.
"A man and a woman, it looks like, from their clothes."

The two skeletons lay close together, with the man's arm
over the woman like he was trying to protect her. Beyond them
another skeleton lay on his face, one arm folded under him.

"So this is what happened to them," Kendra said softly.
"Don't touch anything."

"I've already touched more than I want to. I just want to get
out of here."

The trap door above our heads wasn't nearly as high as the
shaft in the barn, but the ladder leading to it was rotten. The
bottom step crumbled as soon as I put my foot on it.

"It's gotten wet," Kendra said. She touched the ladder and
it started coming apart in her hand like a soggy cardboard box.
"Rain must have leaked through the trap door."

"What if the trap door's rotten, too?"

"Then I guess—"

The lantern went out.

"Oh, no!" Kendra grabbed my arm harder than Dwayne ever
had. "Oh, no! I've got to get out of here. I can't stand being in the
dark. Let me get on your shoulders. Maybe I can reach that door."

Feeling for the wall, I leaned forward slightly and steadied
myself against it. Kendra climbed up my back.

"All right!" she said. "We'll be out of here in a minute.
Brace yourself. I'm going to push hard." Her feet dug into my
shoulders as she heaved against the trap door.

Something cracked. A pile of wood and dirt collapsed on us. We fell to the floor, with Kendra on top of me.

When the dust settled and I could open my eyes, I raised my head enough to see a flood of light and smell fresh air.

"You did it! Hey, you did it!" Kendra didn't answer. "Kendra?"

I crawled out from under the pile of stuff that had fallen on us. Kendra was half-buried under it, her eyes closed. I touched her shoulder. "Kendra? Are you all right?"

She was breathing, but I couldn't wake her up. I piled up some of the fallen wood and managed to climb up it and get my arms over the edge of the hole we had made. I pulled myself up and started to run toward Kendra's house. Then I realized Doc's car was in front of his cottage. I could get to him a lot quicker than I could to Kendra's dad.

Doc opened the door of his cottage when I pounded on it.

"Steve? What's the matter?"

"Kendra's hurt. In a hole over there." I pointed to the cemetery. "Do you have a rope?"

Doc got a rope out of the trunk of his car and ran with me over to the cemetery. He fastened the rope around the Judas Tree and lowered himself into the hole.

"Can I help you bring her up?" I asked.

"I don't think we should move her, Steve." He got out his cell phone and made a call. "We need an ambulance on Williams Road, in the cemetery across from the Rainbow Cottages. And you'd better send the police, too."

⋙⊰⊱⋘

The rest of the afternoon kind of blurred together. I ran and got Kendra's dad. By the time the ambulance got there Kendra was awake. She wanted to get up, but Doc made her lie still. The paramedics strapped her onto a board and lifted her out of the hole, the way I've seen them rescue people on TV. She kept telling them she was fine, but they made her lie down until they checked her over. They looked at her eyes, made her count backwards, asked her what day it was, what her mother's middle name was, and a bunch of other questions.

"She seems to be okay," one of them finally told her dad. "No sign of a concussion or internal injuries. It might be a good idea to take her in for some tests anyway."

"Daddy, please! Let me stay here," she begged. "I've got to see what we've found."

Mr. Jordan agreed she could stay as long as she sat down and wasn't bouncing all over the place. He signed a form and the ambulance left. Doc got a chair from beside the pool at the cottages and set it next to Amanda's tombstone. Kendra sat there, and I sat on the ground beside her.

The sheriff's office sent a deputy to put crime scene tape all over the place and keep people away. But the yellow tape that said **POLICE LINE DO NOT CROSS** only attracted more people. Mr. Philips set up a table in his parking lot right next to the road to sell soft drinks and bottled water. Finally, the deputy had to call in the sheriff himself.

"He'll want to talk to you kids," the deputy said. "Don't go anywhere."

"This'll be great," Kendra said, rubbing her hands together. "Once we tell the sheriff about all that stuff Dwayne stole, he'll never bother us again."

"Do you have to tell?"

She looked at me like I'd suddenly grown another head. "Why would you *not* tell? He'll get in all kinds of trouble."

"Dwayne's got enough trouble already." And I told her about seeing his dad hit him in the parking lot of Philips' store.

"Oh," was all she said.

When the sheriff finally got there, he sat down with Kendra and me and asked us a lot of questions about how we found the tunnel. Her dad stood beside us while we talked. We didn't mention Dwayne by name. I told the sheriff another kid had showed us where to get in.

"Why didn't he come through the tunnel with you?" the sheriff asked.

"He was going fishing. He just showed us and left." That was the truth, kind of. It was hard to keep thinking of answers that made sense but didn't tell everything.

"Why didn't you get out the way you went in?"

"We wanted to explore the rest of the tunnel," I said.

"And then our lantern went out," Kendra added.

The sheriff looked at us the way grown-ups do when they don't quite believe you. "I'll send somebody down there to check out that end of it. Don't want other folks messing around down there."

"It's covered up now," Kendra said. "I don't think anybody will bother it, as long as you keep them out of this end."

The sheriff looked at the barn. It must have seemed too far away, since he would have to walk to get to it. It was a hot day and he was a pretty heavy guy. "I'll talk with you kids about it later. I want you to show me where that other entrance is, though."

"Yes, sir," Kendra and I said. Then we listened while the sheriff and Doc and Mr. Jordan talked about what they ought to do next.

"I guess we should call Reverend Grant," the sheriff said, "since this is on church property."

"It might not be," Kendra said.

"What do you mean?" the sheriff asked. He looked kind of annoyed, like he didn't want this situation to get any more complicated.

"The deacons wouldn't let Amanda be buried in the church cemetery. This wasn't the church's property then. I don't know about now."

"We'll have to check deeds and property lines," Doc said, "but since everybody thinks it belongs to the church, the sheriff's right. It's a good idea to call Reverend Grant."

"And I'm going to call your mothers," Kendra's dad said. Doc let him use his cell phone.

Before long, two hearses from a funeral home in Cadiz pulled up. Before the skeletons were moved, a man from the sheriff's crime lab took a bunch of pictures and somebody else measured the tunnel and marked on a diagram where the bodies were lying. Once they were finished, Doc got his camera and took a bunch more pictures. He was the only one besides the sheriff's people who was allowed to go down into the tunnel.

I was trying to take in everything that was going on and watch for my mom's car at the same time. When she turned onto Williams Road she had to stop because of all the traffic. I saw her and waved. She pulled into Mr. Philips' lot and she and Mrs. Jordan hurried across the cemetery, ignoring Mr. Philips' offer of a free soft drink.

"Steve, are you all right? What on earth is going on?" Mom hugged me. "You're a mess. Where have you been to get in all that red dirt?"

"Just a minute, Mom. I want to see this." I pushed away from her and worked my way through the crowd of people who were watching the men from the funeral home take the bodies out of the tunnel. Each person's remains were placed carefully into a heavy plastic bag, and then carried to one of the hearses.

◈ ❦ ◈

It was late afternoon before the sheriff was finished and people drifted away. The only ones left were Kendra's family and mine, Reverend Grant, and a few of the deacons from the church. And old Mrs. Palmer. I should have known she'd stick her nose in. Kendra and I told our story several times, still leaving Dwayne's name out of it. I could tell Doc wasn't satisfied with our explanation. We would have to tell him the whole truth eventually, but I didn't want my mom to know we had been trapped and could have been down there for several days.

Kendra, Doc, and I stood beside the trapdoor. The sheriff had closed and locked it by having a heavy metal plate laid over it, with steel posts driven into the ground on each side of it and another bar locked in place between them.

"I almost wish we hadn't found them," I said. "I didn't know we would be disturbing them so much."

"But now we know," Kendra said. "We solved the mystery!"

Grampa and Gramma Patterson came up and stood beside us. Reverend Grant and the deacons stood on the other side of the door. My mom and Kendra's parents stood to my left. Her dad was sipping on one of Mr. Philips' soft drinks.

"Professor Crisp," Grampa said, "could you tell if the people were dead before the fire started?"

"I believe they were," Doc said. "All of the bodies showed evidence of bullet wounds."

"Reverend Allen's head was all shot up," I said. I wasn't sure how well I was going to sleep tonight. Creepy movies are fun. Standing beside an actual skeleton ... I shivered.

"The Allens may have tried to hide with the slaves," Doc said, "or they may have been shot and then dumped into the tunnel. Mrs. Allen did not die immediately. I think she was trying to crawl down the tunnel."

Mrs. Palmer held Doc's hand. "It's horrible," she said, and everybody nodded. "Standing here in this peaceful afternoon shade, it seems impossible that somebody could have done something so violent, almost in the shadow of the church."

"How do you think it happened, Professor?" Reverend Grant asked.

"From what I've seen," Doc said, "I think it happened like this ..."

As he talked, my imagination turned his words into a story I hoped I'd be able to write someday.

CHAPTER 20

THE SOUND OF singing faded under the drumming of hoofbeats, growing louder as the horses drew nearer. Laura Allen pulled back the calico curtain covering the small window in the east end of the house and glanced out. In the twilight it was hard to tell exactly how many riders were approaching. There were too many for it to be a peaceful visit. Of that she was sure.

"Matthew! We have to hide!" she said. "Everybody, into the tunnel. Quickly!"

The four escaping slaves, two men and two women, hurried down the ladder.

"Be absolutely still," Laura warned them, then slid the trapdoor in place. Their bed, raised to allow room under it for Amanda's trundle bed, stood over the trapdoor. The trundle bed, unused for several weeks now, served a purpose. Through a small hole in the trapdoor, an iron bar could be inserted and used to slide the small bed in and out, hiding the trapdoor from all but the most inquisitive eyes, and allowing everyone in the house to hide in the tunnel, if need be, and still hide the door.

Matthew Allen still had not risen from his place at the table in front of the fireplace. He had seemed so distant, so disconnected, in the weeks since Amanda died of the influenza. He had worked so hard carving her tombstone, but now that task was finished and he had nothing to occupy him.

"Matthew, hurry!" his wife urged.

"If we all go down in the tunnel," he replied softly, "they'll just burn the place over us."

"Then what are you going to do?" Laura asked. "There are too many of them. We can't fight them."

"Laura, you know I wouldn't fight them, even if I could. I'm going to follow the teaching of the Gospel of Matthew—to be as harmless as a dove and as wise as a serpent. I'm going to talk to them, invite them in to search the house if they wish. They'll find you knitting and me reading my Bible."

"But do you think they are not coming to kill us?" Laura's voice rose in panic as the horsemen drew up around the house.

"If they be determined to do so, then nothing we can do will stop them," her husband said calmly, standing to face the door.

"Can't we try?" Laura demanded. "Must we just sit here and let them do this? You have a gun!"

"Which I use only for hunting. You know I would never turn it against another human being. We are in the right and we know that a mansion is prepared for us. Amanda waits there for us." He held his wife tightly for a moment, then strode to the door. Mrs. Allen sat down in a rocker by the fire and took out her knitting, which was always by that chair so she could work on it in any spare moments she might have. She forced her shaking hands to knit and purl.

"Hallo, the house!" a voice called from outside.

Matthew Allen opened the door and stepped out onto the front porch. "Good evening, gentlemen," he said. "May I be of some assistance?"

In front of the house a dozen gray-clad men sat on sweaty horses, whose breath came out in little clouds. Other men had stationed themselves on the sides and the back of the house to prevent escapes. Their faces were indistinct, hidden in the growing darkness under hat brims. Two more men with them wore civilian clothes.

"Be you the Reverend Matthew Allen?" the leader asked.

"I am he," Reverend Allen replied.

"We'll waste no time mincing words, sir," the leader said. "We know that you are, and have been, hiding runaway slaves and helping them find their way north. We aim to put a stop to that."

Matthew Allen shrugged his shoulders and spread his hands as if to show that they were empty. "I know nothing about this."

One of the civilians spoke sharply. "You're violating the commandment against lying, Reverend. You claim to be obeying divine law in not returning slaves. If you break one commandment, you break them all. You yourself have said that from the pulpit."

"Good evening, Deacon Clay. Are you the Judas who

brought this mob here? I welcome you none the less. If you and your friends would like to come in ..."

The leader of the riders drew his pistol. "We aim to." He fired a shot, which knocked Reverend Allen back against the doorpost. Two more shots, fired by the horsemen on both sides of him, made certain the minister was dead.

"Let's finish this quickly." The leader dismounted and stepped over Reverend Allen's body. "No survivors. We're here to show 'em we mean business."

He was the first one through the door but jerked to a halt and found himself staring into the barrel of a rifle.

"I could kill you," Laura Allen said, aiming at his head. "But what good would it do? It wouldn't bring my husband back. It wouldn't stop your men from killing me."

"We're soldiers, ma'am," the leader said, trying to steady his quavering voice. "We do what we have to, even if we don't like it."

"But *why* do you have to?" Laura Allen asked as tears spilled over and began to run down her pale cheeks.

"To defend our cause."

"Is a cause worth defending when it makes you skulk around in the dark, hunting down innocent people, killing unarmed men and women?"

"Your side does no better," the man snapped back.

"I am only on the side of freedom and peace," Laura Allen said. "You have a family, don't you?"

The man nodded.

"I'm sure they love you, just as every dead soldier has someone who loves him. Why should I put them through the agony of losing you? Your death would change nothing. Your life might, eventually."

As she lowered the rifle, the shattering of the glass in the window caused her to turn in that direction. The man at the window fired one shot at her, just as a soldier who had eased into position behind his commander in the doorway fired another.

"No!" Ezra Clay screamed from the yard. "Oh, God, no!"

⊰⊱

"It's all so tragic," Mrs. Palmer said. "Six lives snuffed out."

"Seven, actually," Gramma said quietly.

"What do you mean, Ruth?" Mrs. Palmer asked.

"A seventh person eventually died as a result of this incident," Gramma said, and she quickly told Ezra Clay's story.

"Because someone in our family was responsible for what happened here," Gramma said, "Henry and I believe we ought to do more than just feel sorry about it."

"But what can anyone do after so long a time?" Mrs. Palmer said. I hated to hear her saying the same thing I'd told Kendra.

"We can't change the past," Grampa said, "but we can admit our ancestors were wrong, and we can make up for it in some way, however small. We've talked with Reverend Grant, and what we'd like to do is have a funeral for the Allens and the others. The Allens ought to be buried next to their little girl, and those poor slaves should be properly buried here, too. I'm just sorry we don't know their names. We're willing to pay for the funeral and the tombstones ourselves."

"That's a beautiful idea, Henry," one of the deacons said. "But the church was responsible for driving Reverend Allen out, and as a member of the church I'd like to do something about that. I'd be happy to contribute to those expenses, too."

Several more people promised to help pay for the funeral.

"I'll announce it in church tomorrow," Reverend Grant said. "I'm sure many of our people would like to be part of this."

I looked at Kendra. She was smiling and crying at the same time. When she looked back at me, I rubbed my eye, like I had something in it.

Mrs. Palmer began singing 'Swing Low, Sweet Chariot'. I was surprised at what a beautiful voice she had. Doc and Reverend Grant joined her, and then everyone started singing.

CHAPTER 21

"ARE YOU GOING out again?" Mom said as I opened the back door after supper. "Why don't you stay in, after all the excitement today?"

"I'm too hyped up to sit still," I said. "I won't be long."

Mom put her hands on my shoulders and drew me close to her. "I'm going to worry about you now every time you set foot out of the house because you and Kendra got trapped in that tunnel. That kind of thing isn't supposed to happen in our safe little part of the world. It scares me to think there's somebody like Dwayne around here."

I had had to tell her the whole story. "I don't think he's evil, Mom. Anyway, I just want to ask Doc about a couple of things. I can't stay in the house for the rest of my life."

"Well, if you're not home in an hour, I'll call the police."

I could sense her watching me through the living room window as I walked past the church, turned right, and headed toward the 'Rainbow Cottages'. Even though I knew I was out of her sight by the time I got past the church, I felt like she could still see me when I left the road, cut across the cemetery past the Allens' house and Amanda's grave, and headed for the barn.

This is crazy, I told myself as I sat in the barn behind the remaining wall of a horse's stall. *Why do I think Dwayne is going to come back tonight? He said he wouldn't be back till Monday, and he's probably mean enough to leave us down in that hole for a couple of days. And what do I say to him if he does show up?*

I only had to wait about fifteen minutes before I heard somebody come into the barn. Dwayne shoved the grain bin aside, knelt down, and looked into the shaft. "Kendra, Steve, I'm ba-a-a-ack," he called in a mocking voice.

"I figured you would be," I said, standing up.

Dwayne jerked so violently he almost fell into the hole. "What the ...? How the ...?" He unleashed his usual string of cuss words.

"I didn't think you were really mean enough to leave us down there till Monday," I said.

"I just came back to check on my comics. Why would I care what happens to you?" He stood up and made a fist with his right hand. "How did you get out?"

"This is part of a tunnel that runs up to where a house used to be on Williams Road. We dug through the part that had caved in and got out the other end."

Dwayne took a threatening step toward me. "Have you told anybody how you got down here?"

"Not the whole story. We've talked to Professor Crisp and my mom." This didn't seem like the best time to mention the sheriff. "Nobody's been in this end of the tunnel yet. They'll want to take a look at it tomorrow, though."

"They'll find my stuff!" Dwayne doubled up his other fist.

I wanted to move away from him, but my back was against the stall. "Not if you get it out tonight."

He shook his head like he couldn't believe what he was hearing. "You're not gonna snitch on me? Mr. Goody-goody, who wouldn't let me get out of the bookstore with one stolen comic, is gonna let me walk out of here with a box full of 'em and not say anything? What's the catch?"

"Dwayne, I'm really getting tired of this. I don't know why you don't like me. I've never done or said anything to hurt you. I even helped you out in the bookstore. I don't think your dad would have been too happy if you got caught shoplifting."

"Stop actin' like some kind of saint, Patterson! The reason I got in trouble was 'cause of you and that nosy Kendra."

He took another step toward me. I had to force myself not to run. I suddenly realized that, if I had misjudged Dwayne, there was nothing to stop him from beating me up, maybe even throwing me down into the tunnel again. And the other end, under the Allens' house, was sealed up tight now.

But I had to do this, no matter what happened to me. The Allens stood up for what they thought was right and paid a greater price than I ever would.

"Come on, Dwayne!" I said as loud as I could. He stopped. "You were *stealing* something. We couldn't just stand there and let you get away with it. If we hadn't spotted you then, somebody else would have sooner or later. You can't keep doing that forever without getting caught."

"I've had pretty good luck so far. You saw my collection." He actually sounded proud of himself.

"Yeah, but you can't even let anybody know you have them. You have to sneak out here and crawl down into a hole in the ground to look at them. Do you want to do that for the rest of your life?"

Dwayne stepped back. He tried to put his usual sneer back on his face, but it didn't convince me. "Hey," he said, "my old man says you have to grab what you want. Most of us aren't as lucky as you."

"Me, lucky? Where did you get that idea?"

"You got that story published in the newspaper, and they put your picture up in the display case at school. You got me out in that ball game. All I needed was a lousy base hit to be the hero, but, no, you had to make like the ace relief pitcher. And you always make good grades. And people like you."

I shook my head. Whose life was he talking about? "Is that really what my life looks like to you? Don't you know my dad left when I was five? I didn't even get a birthday card from him last year. Nothing can make up for that. I can't tell you how much it hurts."

"Not as much as it hurts to have my old man slappin' me around." The anger drained out of Dwayne's voice. "Yeah, okay, I'm sorry about your dad, I mean. I knew your folks were divorced, but I hate my old man so much that looked like one more way you were lucky, not havin' somebody beatin' up on you."

You do a pretty good job of that, I thought. "Can't you tell him how you feel about it, like you don't understand why he hits you?"

Dwayne gave a snort. "I know why he hits me. Because he's a jerk. That's why I liked havin' this place, so I could just get away from him and everybody else for a while."

"Well, I think you'll want to get that stuff out of the tunnel and take the ladder back to Kendra's garage."

"Are you givin' me orders?" Dwayne flared up.

I held my ground. "Just a warning. People are going to be looking around down here tomorrow. That's all I'm saying. I think you ought to give the comics back, but I can't make you. I'm not going to help you move the stuff, because it's stolen and I don't want to know anything about where it is."

"Fair enough." Dwayne picked up the ladder and lowered it into the shaft.

"Hey, Dwayne."

"Now what?"

"Would you like to come over to my house tomorrow to ..." I started to say 'to get away from your dad for a while,' but I caught myself. "... to play some ball?"

Dwayne shook his head and almost smiled. "You know, Patterson, I never have been able to figure you out."

"You don't know anything about me. You've never tried to find out. You just decided you didn't like me. I don't know you well enough to know whether I like you or not. I'm willing to find out. Do you want to come over?"

◈ ◖◗ ◈

"You invited *Dwayne* over here?" I thought my mom was going to explode when I told her that night. "Don't you realize that boy tried to kill you?"

"Come on, Mom. He didn't hurt me." At least not in the tunnel. "He was just trying to scare Kendra and me. He came back to let us out."

"I don't care. I don't want him in this house."

"You know, Mom, when you taught my Sunday School class last year, you told us to love our enemies. Didn't you mean it?"

She looked up over the pile of laundry she was folding. "I don't know of anywhere in the Bible that it says to invite your enemy over to your house to play ball. You can love him without getting that close to him."

"But you don't understand. I think Dwayne ... needs help."

"You're right about that. Anybody who steals stuff and traps two kids in a tunnel certainly does need help. In a few more years he's going to be stealing cars and who knows what else."

"I might be getting into trouble, too, if my dad or you treated me the way Dwayne's dad treats him."

Mom put a towel into the laundry basket, but she didn't pick up anything else to fold. She gave me her full attention. "What do you mean?"

It's hard to tell an adult that another adult is hurting a kid. In school we've been told that people aren't supposed to touch us in the wrong places or hit us and, if they do, we're supposed to tell somebody—a teacher, a minister, a parent. But when you find yourself in that situation, you don't know what to say because you don't know how the adult is going to react. I decided I had to trust my mom.

"Dwayne's dad hits him. I saw him do it. He hit him hard."

"Oh, that poor child. What do you think you can do about it?"

"I just thought Dwayne could use a friend."

CHAPTER 22

ON SUNDAY AFTERNOON Kendra, Dwayne, and I played ball for a while. Actually, Dwayne and I played. He was the catcher on his team, so I got a chance to practice my pitching. Kendra spent most of the time sitting on the porch glaring at me. She hardly said anything. She wasn't openly rude to Dwayne—I had to give her credit for that—but we could both tell she did not want him there.

My mom watched us more closely than she needed to. Any time I looked at the house I saw her face in one window or another. Finally she stuck her head out the front door. "Seventh inning stretch! Do you kids want something to drink?"

"We have root beer," I said to Dwayne. I had gone to Philips' store earlier that afternoon and bought a couple of cans.

"Good, you owe me one." He punched me on the arm, but not hard. "I didn't steal those."

As we started up the steps Kendra brushed past us. "I'm going home. See you later." I think she meant the 'you' to apply only to me. Or maybe she was talking to my mom. It was hard to tell, since she wouldn't look at any of us.

The way Mom looked at me, though, she didn't have to say anything. I could read a whole lecture in her eyes. *You're going to lose Kendra as a friend. She's been your best friend all these years. Are you sure Dwayne's worth it? You don't know if you can trust him.*

I didn't have an answer for that. I just felt like this was what I had to do.

"Could we look at your baseball cards?" Dwayne asked. "I'd really like to see that Chipper Jones rookie card."

While Dwayne and I were looking at my cards the phone rang. "It's for you, Steve," Mom said.

When I put the phone to my ear Kendra said, "You might

like to know that the sheriff and Doc and some other people are down at the Allens' house. I saw them out our kitchen window. I'm going down there." Then she hung up.

"You didn't get to say much," Dwayne said as he held up Chipper's rookie card in its plastic sleeve.

"Oh ... I ... uh ..."

Dwayne put the card down. "That was Kendra, wasn't it? She's mad at you for invitin' me over here."

"No. She didn't say anything about that. Honest."

"Well, she's mad at you. And she doesn't want any part of me." He got up. "I'd better just go."

"Dwayne, no."

"Hey, it's okay, Steve. I know what's going on. You two've been friends for a long time. I guess there's no room for—"

"Hey, no, don't go. Kendra can't tell me who I can invite over to my house and who I can't." I put a hand on his shoulder to stop him. "In fact, come on. Let's get going."

"Where're we goin'?"

"I want you to see what Kendra and I found yesterday. It's pretty amazing."

Dwayne and I cut through Kendra's yard and her neighbor's yard and behind the church to the cemetery. I had never done that before because Mom told me not to, but, like Dwayne said, it was shorter. As we came up to Amanda's grave Doc waved. Kendra, standing beside him, gave no sign she had even seen us. She was talking to a woman I didn't know.

"Steve, you're just in time," Doc said. "There's a reporter here who'd like to talk to you. She wants to interview the people who found the bodies and get a picture for the paper."

Dwayne hung back as Doc took me over to the reporter and introduced me. She began asking questions. I noticed she used a notebook like mine.

"I'm still not clear on something," she finally said. "Exactly how did you find the entrance to the tunnel?"

I looked at Kendra. "He's your friend," she said, "not mine."

The way she said it made me as mad as what she said. I turned back to the reporter. "Actually Dwayne here found it." I turned to point to Dwayne, but he was halfway back up the hill.

"Dwayne, wait!"

"I'll see you in the paper, Steverino."

I ran part of the way after him. "No, come here."

Dwayne trudged back down the hill to where I was standing. "Why are you bein' nice to me, Patterson? Do you just feel sorry for me?" His mouth was starting to curl up in his familiar sneer. "'Cause if you are, I don't need that."

"Dwayne, think about it. If you hadn't found that tunnel, we wouldn't have been in it. And if you hadn't come back to let us out last night, we wouldn't be standing here right now. I don't believe you're as bad a person as you think you are."

"Is that what you call a left-handed compliment? Like 'you sweat less than any fat kid I know'?" He smiled and punched me on the arm again.

I rubbed my arm. "Okay, one thing. If we have any chance to be friends, you've got to stop doing that."

"Sorry. It's a habit. There's a lotta hittin' in my family. I guess you know that." We turned and walked down to Amanda's grave. "Listen, I'm gonna pay you back that three dollars. I promise."

Kendra and the reporter were looking down into the tunnel under the Allens' house. The reporter took a couple of pictures.

"This is Dwayne Mitchell," I told the reporter. "He discovered the other end of the tunnel down in the barn. If he hadn't, we wouldn't have known the tunnel was there, much less found the bodies." I was really talking to Kendra now.

"I've seen that end of the tunnel," the reporter said. "How did you get into it?"

"We used a ladder," I said. "One that belongs to Kendra's family."

"It's back in their garage now," Dwayne added.

The reporter took several pictures of us, one with us around Amanda's tombstone and a couple of us around the edge of the trapdoor. "One more," she finally said. "Let's try it with you sitting on the edge of the opening with your legs hanging over. And let's put the taller boy in the middle this time."

"I wonder if this'll get in the display case at school next fall," Dwayne said as we smiled at the camera. At least he and I were smiling.

⮜⳥⳨⮞

We had to wait until Wednesday to see the story. The Cadiz paper still comes out only once a week. But we got a nice headline:

LOCAL YOUTHS SOLVE CENTURY-OLD SLAYINGS

They used the picture of the three of us around Amanda's tombstone.

"I guess a hole in the ground didn't show up as well," Kendra said as we read it together. She was back to speaking to me.

The story itself didn't exactly satisfy either Kendra or me. It left out some details we felt were important, but at least it didn't get anything wrong. And it didn't give Dwayne too much credit.

CHAPTER 23

"So, WHAT ARE you going to do with the rest of your summer?" Mom asked Kendra and me as she was leaving to go back to work. She had come home for lunch to bring copies of the paper and a congratulations card people in the hardware store signed for us. "It may be kind of boring after all this excitement."

"Heck, no," I said. "I want to write a story based on what we found out about the Allens. And I want to work on my change-up and throwing to first on bunts."

"Just don't use one of my rose bushes for your first baseman."

"I won't have to, Mom. Dwayne's coming over again, okay?"

Mom sighed. "If you can be a friend to that boy after what he did, you're a better person than I am. Just stay out of barns when he's around. Will you keep an eye on them, Kendra?"

"I'll keep an eye on Steve. Dwayne can take care of himself."

"That's part of his problem," Mom said. "His parents aren't doing their job. The wife of a man at the store works in Social Services. I'll talk to her. Maybe we can do something for Dwayne."

Kendra shook her head. "My dad says he just needs a good swift kick in the—"

"He's gotten too many of those already," I said.

After my mom left, Kendra turned to me, "How'd the visit with your dad go last night? You haven't said a word about it."

"What's to say? It was awful." Totally out of the blue, my dad had called yesterday from Gramma and Grampa's house. He was in town and wanted to see me. I guess he expected me to be happy, but why should I be?

"Mom dropped me off at Gramma and Grampa's," I said, "to have supper with them and Dad."

"Your mom didn't go?"

"She didn't want to see him. I guess I didn't have as good a reason as she did, not to see him."

"Why did he come back after three years?"

"To tell us that he's gotten a job in Miami and he wants me to come down there and spend some time with him. Maybe this summer, if he gets settled in. Maybe over Christmas."

Kendra sat up excitedly. "That'd be too cool. All those beaches and stuff."

"Kendra, it's my dad talking. All he does is talk. It's not going to happen."

"Hey, maybe he's trying to change. Maybe he's sorry he hasn't been a very good dad lately."

"Well, he's changed in one way."

"What?"

"He had his new wife with him."

"His new wife?" Kendra almost jumped out of her chair.

"Yeah. I've got a stepmother."

"And he hadn't told anybody?"

"Not until Friday. That's why Mom was so upset when we were looking through those pictures at Gramma's and Grampa's."

"What's she like?"

"She acts like she's about eighteen. Hair so blonde it's almost white. Clothes so tight she could hardly sit down. And she kept talking about how she 'knows she can't replace my mom, but we're going to be such great friends'." I mimicked her voice. "I thought I was going to be sick."

"Do you *have* to go down there and stay with him?"

"Mom said he's supposed to have regular visits with me. That was part of the agreement when they got divorced. She's going to talk to her lawyer and see what we have to do."

"What does it feel like to have a stepmother?"

"Look, I don't want to talk about it. She may be married to my dad, but she's no kind of mother to me. Just like he's not much of a dad."

"But—"

"Hey, drop it, okay? Read your book."

⇜ ⟅⟆ ⇝

About half an hour later Kendra was reading about Sherlock Holmes and some guys with red hair. I was working on my story about the

Allens. We looked up when Doc's car pulled into the driveway. We hadn't seen him since Sunday. I didn't have to be Sherlock Holmes or Dr. Whatzit to figure out, from the boxes piled in the back seat, that he was going somewhere. Probably back to Indiana.

"Good afternoon," he said with a smile, getting out of the car.

"Hi," we said.

"Why so glum?" Doc asked. "Was it something I said?"

"Are you leaving?" Kendra pointed to the boxes in his car.

"Yes and no."

"What's that supposed to mean?" I said. "Either you are or you aren't."

"Let's talk a short walk," Doc said.

"Grown-ups always change the subject when they don't want to talk to kids about something," I said.

"Yeah," Kendra said, "especially something that matters to the kids."

"I'm not changing the subject," Doc said. "I just want to explain how someone can be leaving and maybe not leaving at the same time. Teachers and writers try to *show* something, not *tell* it. That's what I want to do. So, come on."

We walked to the corner and turned left on Williams Road. That took us up to the very top of the hill overlooking the lake. We passed several new homes, none of them quite finished, before Doc stopped in front of the old Bradford house.

"Here it is," he said.

"This old dump?" I said. "This is what you want to show us?"

"It's actually a charming place with a lot of potential," Doc said. "That's why Leona and I are going to buy it."

"What?" Kendra and I said together.

"It will make an excellent bed-and-breakfast place," Doc said. "Leona and I both have some money we can invest, so we've formed a partnership. Come on. Take a look."

We followed him up onto the porch. It ran around three sides of the house. On one side a big swing hung from the ceiling. Doc invited us to sit in it. From there we looked out over the other side of the hill and the lake beyond.

"Wow! What a view!" Kendra said.

"Exactly," Doc said. "This is why we think people will want to stay here in a bed-and-breakfast."

"What's a bed-and-breakfast?" I asked.

"It's a kind of hotel, except it's in a house, usually an old house, and there are only a few rooms. There will be five rooms in this one. Tourists stay in them, just like they would a hotel, but it's more like being a guest in someone's home."

"Are you going to live here?" I asked. "Or is Mrs. Palmer?" The thought of having old lady Palmer as a neighbor was more than I could stand at that moment.

"There are still a lot of details to work out," Doc said. "I have to go back to Indiana and see about selling my house and see if I can take early retirement from the college. And there's also the question of the bookstore in Cadiz."

"Mr. Morse's store?" Kendra said. "What about it?"

"Mr. Morse is Mrs. Bradford's younger brother, her only surviving relative. He inherited the house and land. He's made so much money from selling the land, he wants to retire to Florida. He's willing to sell the bookstore as well as the house. I've always thought I'd like to own a bookstore."

"What'll you do with the baseball cards?" I asked.

"I don't know anything about comics or baseball cards, so I would sell those off to some other dealer. I just want to concentrate on old books."

Bummer. I knew I could never afford the really rare cards, but I loved looking at them and dreaming. Once in a while I could buy an older card with birthday or Christmas money.

"Of course," Doc said, "it would be a big job. I'd like to put in some different shelves, clean and paint the place. And get that awful cigarette smell out. I would need some help. I'd be willing to trade some cards for some work."

"That'd be great!" I said. Then I had an idea, an inspiration. "You know, Dwayne Mitchell collects old comic books."

"'Collects' them?" Kendra hooted. "That's one way to put it."

"Put a sock in it, Kendra. Could you use two workers, Doc? Dwayne's a big strong kid."

"Funny you should mention comic books. Mr. Morse said he found a plastic container of them by the back door a couple of days ago, ones that had been stolen from the store. Do you know anything about that?"

"We don't read comic books," I said.

"Just mystery books," Kendra added.

"Well, I could use some good workers," Doc said. "And there are a lot more mystery novels in the store than I need."

"I only work for cash," Kendra said.

"You drive a hard bargain, but okay. I'm really excited about this. I feel like there are lots of opportunities for me here, to write, to get to know some new people, to coach some baseball. But I do need to settle things in Indiana. It will take some time before the paperwork is approved on this house and the bookstore. I'm coming back, though, in a couple of weeks, for the big day."

"What big day?" Kendra and I asked.

"That's the other thing I wanted to tell you about. The mayor and some others in the community heard about what you found. They want to have a memorial service. One member of the church is interested in having the Allens' house rebuilt. Leona contacted the State Historical Commission on Monday. They're sending someone to look over the site as a possible monument. Since we're so close to the lake and all those tourists, the Allens' place could become an attraction. And an important historical site."

"Can they do that on church property?" I asked.

"It's not clear who owns that land," Doc said. "The state may take it over. The last known owners were the Allens, and they died without wills."

"Holy cow! We really did start something, didn't we?" Kendra said.

"You did," Doc said. "That's one of the exciting things about investigating problems. You never know where you'll end up."

"You started it, Doc," I said. "If you hadn't put the flowers on Amanda's grave, Kendra and I would never have looked at it."

"Now, if you're going to be right here all the time," Kendra said, "you can put flowers on her grave any time you want to."

"I could, and I will," Doc said, "but Amanda's not going to be lonely any more, thanks to you two."

END

᭰ᨀᨂ᭰

❧ ᘓᘔ ❧

FOLLOW THE DRINKING GOURD

Follow the drinking gourd!
Follow the drinking gourd.
For the old man is awaiting
     for to carry you to freedom
If you follow the drinking gourd.

When the sun comes back and the first quail calls,
Follow the drinking gourd,
For the old man is awaiting
     for to carry you to freedom
If you follow the drinking gourd.

The riverbank makes a very good road,
The dead trees will show you the way,
Left foot, peg foot traveling on,
Following the drinking gourd.

The river ends between two hills,
Follow the drinking gourd,
There's another river on the other side,
Follow the drinking gourd.

Where the great big river meets the little river,
Follow the drinking gourd,
The old man is awaiting
     for to carry you to freedom
If you follow the drinking gourd

❧ ᘓᘔ ❧

UNDERGROUND RAILROAD 1860

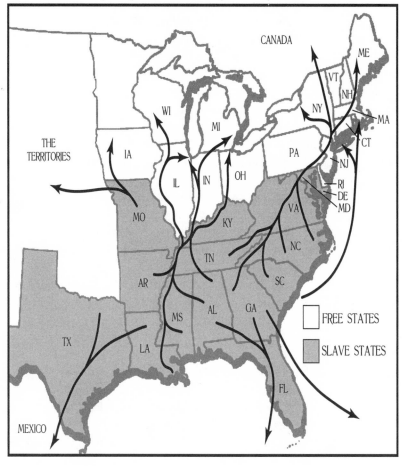

CANADA

ME

VT

NH

NY

MA

THE
TERRITORIES

IA

WI

MI

CT

PA

NJ

IL

IN

OH

RI
DE
MD

MO

KY

VA

TN

NC

AR

SC

MS

AL

GA

TX

LA

☐ FREE STATES

▨ SLAVE STATES

FL

MEXICO

A NOTE ON SLAVERY IN THE UNITED STATES

It's hard to imagine one person "owning" another one, isn't it? Today we're proud that we live in a free country and that our laws guarantee rights to everyone, regardless of their race, their religion, or where they came from.

But it hasn't always been that way, in America or in other countries. For thousands of years, people who were defeated in war were captured and forced to work as slaves for those who had conquered them. They could be sold or moved anywhere their captors wanted, just like any other property. This system seemed natural in those days because no one had ever known anything different and because they had no machinery to do their work. They needed people to do hard physical labor, and people didn't always want to do it, so slaves were forced to work.

Even after Christianity began to preach, as Paul says, that there was no difference between slave or free, Jew or Greek, male or female, the idea of the equality of all people did not spread rapidly. As long as there was a need for people to do the hardest work and as long as there were places to conquer, slavery was an important part of society. Once machines began to be used, though, the need for slaves lessened. But—ironically—it was a machine, the cotton gin, that made the growing of cotton profitable in the American South and dramatically increased the need for slaves in that area.

The story told in this book is fiction, but it is based on the very real fact that Africans were held in slavery in this country until 1865 (and in other places even after that). This outline will help you to see some significant developments in the history of slavery in America, from the arrival of a handful of slaves in 1502 to the point, just over 350 years later, when there were about 4,000,000 African slaves in the U. S.

Most slaves suffered harsh conditions and lived with the knowledge that they, or their families, could be separated and sold at any time. If they tried to escape, they could be hunted like criminals, as the reward posters below reveal. In most places it was against the law to teach a slave to read or write. By the early 1800s a number of people, black and white, were speaking out against the injustice and inhumanity of slavery. Most countries in western Europe abolished slavery by the 1830s, and some Americans argued that this country ought to follow that example. But the issue created bitter division. People who spoke out against slavery, as Reverend Allen did in this story, often met harsh criticism, or were attacked.

Today, 150 years after the abolition of slavery in America, historians and sociologists still debate the impact it had on the country then, and the lingering effects it may still have on all of us—black and white—now. I hope this story can help you imagine what it was like to live in America when some people were slaves, and understand why that fact still matters so much to so many people.

•African slaves accompanied the first Spanish and French explorers to the New World, as early as 1502.

•The first slave laborers were brought to Virginia in 1619, the year before the Mayflower landed at Plymouth Rock.

•For over a century slavery was legal in all the American colonies. It was gradually abolished in the Northern colonies/states. Vermont did away with it in 1777. Ohio abolished it in 1803, Indiana in 1816, New York in 1827, and Connecticut in 1848.

•Some Northern states passed what were known as gradual emancipation laws, allowing children of slaves to be free when they reached a certain age, usually 28. This was done so slaves would not be thrown out with no way to support themselves

•Eli Whitney's invention of a machine known as the cotton gin in 1793 made the growing of cotton on a large scale profitable. This increased the demand for slaves in the South.

•The U. S. Constitution prohibited the importation of slaves from Africa after 1808. The United States and Great Britain set up naval patrols along the west coast of Africa to stop slave ships.

•Slavery was not common in parts of the South where cotton was not grown, especially in mountainous areas of eastern Kentucky and Tennessee, and in western Virginia and North Carolina.

•In 1817 the American Colonization Society was founded. Its purpose was to return African slaves to Africa. During the 1820s about 1,400 freed slaves were sent to the new country of Liberia.

•Several slave revolts or uprisings occurred in the early 1800s: one in Virginia in 1802, another in South Carolina in 1822, and Nat Turner's in Virginia in 1831.

•In 1820 Missouri came into the Union as a slave state, with Maine joining as a free state, under the "Missouri Compromise."

•By 1827 a movement to abolish slavery in the United States was gaining strength. African-Americans such as James W. C. Pennington, David Walker and Peter Williams played prominent roles.

•In 1833 William Lloyd Garrison and others founded the American Anti-Slavery Society. Garrison published a paper called the *Liberator*.

•Public sentiment in the North did not always favor the abolitionists. Abolitionist leaders were attacked, even killed, in New York in 1834, in Illinois in 1837, and in Philadelphia in 1838.

•In 1837 free African-Americans were denied the right to vote in Pennsylvania and Michigan.

•Sojourner Truth, a woman who had escaped from slavery, began lecturing in favor of abolition in 1843.

•In 1854 the Kansas-Nebraska Act repealed the Missouri Compromise and opened the western territories of the United States to slavery, if people in a particular territory favored it.

•During the 1850s Harriet Tubman, who had escaped slavery in Maryland, helped over 300 slaves escape north along the Underground Railroad. According to those who knew her, Tubman threatened to shoot any slaves who lost their nerve and wanted to turn back. During the Civil War she worked as a spy for the Union.

•Dred Scott, whose master had died, sued for freedom on the grounds that he and his master had lived for a number of years in places where slavery was illegal. In 1857 the Supreme Court ruled, 7-2, that Scott could not sue because no slave or descendant of a slave could be a U. S. citizen, so he must remain a slave.

•The Kansas-Nebraska Act and the Dred Scott decision were two factors that created new tensions over slavery and prompted Abraham Lincoln to begin his political career.

•In October, 1859 abolitionist John Brown led a raid on a government arsenal at Harper's Ferry, Virginia, hoping to seize weapons to support a slave rebellion. The raid failed. Brown was tried and executed. As he died, he predicted a civil war would be necessary to end slavery in the U. S.

•According to the Historical Statistics of the United States (1970), fewer than one-fourth of white Southerners owned slaves.

•Most Southerners who did own slaves owned fewer than 5; only 1 percent owned more than 100.

•The total number of slaves in the South in 1860 was under 4,000,000. Only in South Carolina and Mississippi did slaves outnumber free persons.

Reward Posters

Even before the Underground Railroad became active, slaves tried to run away to free territories. Their owners often printed and distributed posters describing the runaways, offering rewards for their capture and return. Since they had no cameras or other ways of providing pictures of the slaves, the owners—"subscribers" in the posters—usually gave detailed descriptions. Here are the texts of five posters, with the original spellings and punctuation:

$50 Reward

Run away on the 17th night of April last, from the subscribers living in Mecklenburg County N.C. near Charlote, two likely young negro fellows (viz.) Jacob and Stephen. Jacob is aboot 23 years of age, stout made, dark complected and his gums of a blackish colour. Stephen is about 21 years of age, stout made, dark complected, and not so thick set as Jacob with a small tear on his under lip cut with a pen knife, and a scar on his throat. They set out for Philadelphia, and was last June between Petersburg and Richmond, on their way; they are both smart and active. We will give the above reward and pay all reasonable expences to any persons that will apprehend and confine them, in any Jail so as we get them, or deliver them to us in Charlotte, or 25 dollars for either, and if you secure them write to Charlotte or advertise them in the Richmond Enquirer untill we get them.

Zenas Alexander
George Alexander
January, 2d 1817.

$100 Reward

Ran away from my farm, near Buena Vista P. O., Prince George's County, Maryland, on the first day of April, 1855, my servant MATHEW TURNER. He is about five feet six or eight inches high; weighs from one hundred and sixty to one hundred and eighty pounds; he is very black, and has a remarkably thick upper lip and neck; looks as if his eyes are half closed; walks slow, and talks and laughs loud. I will give One Hundred Dollars reward to whoever will secure him in jail, so that I get him again, no matter where taken.

Marcus Du Val
Buena Vista P. O., MD.
May 10, 1855

$150 Reward

Ran away from the subscriber, on the night of the 2d instant, a negro man, who calls himself Henry May, about 22 years old, 5 feet 6 or 8 inches high, ordinary color, rather chunky built, bushy head, and has it divided mostly on one side, and keeps it very nicely combed; has been raised in the house, and is a first rate dining-room servant, and was in a tavern in Louisville for 18 months. I expect he is now in Louisville trying to make his escape to a free state (in all probability to Cincinnati, Ohio). Perhaps he may try to get employment on a steamboat. He is a good cook, and is handy in any capacity as a house servant. Had on when he left, a dark cassinett coat, and dark striped cassinett pantaloons, new—he had other clothing. I will give $50 reward if taken in Louisville; 100 dollars if taken one hundred miles from Louisville in this State, and 150 dollars if taken out of this State, and delivered to me, or secured in any jail so that I can get him again.

William Burke
Bardstown, Ky., September 3d, 1838

$20 Reward

Ran away from the Subscriber, on the 22nd December last, his negro man MARTIN, aged about 23 years. He has a pleasing countenance, round face, is quick spoken, and can tell a very plausible story; he is a shining black, stout built, with large limbs, short fingers, and small feet; the toe next to his great toe has been mashed off. The above reward will be paid on his delivery to me, or at any Jail in North Carolina.

James R. Wood
Wadesboro, Feb. 5, 1844

$200 REWARD

Ran Away from the subscriber, on the night of Thursday, the 30th of September, FIVE NEGRO SLAVES, To-wit, one Negro man, his wife and three children.

The man is a black negro, full height, very erect, his face a little thin. He is about forty years of age, and calls himself Washington Reed, and is known by the name of Washington. He is probably well dressed, possibly takes with him an ivory-headed cane, and is of good address. Several of his teeth are gone.

Mary, his wife, is about thirty years of age, a bright mulatto woman, and quite stout and strong.

The oldest of the children is a boy, of the name of FIELDING, twelve years of age, a dark mulatto, with heavy eyelids. He probably wore a new cloth cap.

MATILDA, the second child, is a girl, six years of age, rather a dark mulatto, but a bright and smart looking child.

MALCOLM, the youngest, is a boy, four years old, a lighter mulatto than the last, and about equally as bright. He probably also wore a cloth cap. If examined, he will be found to have a swelling at the navel.

Washington and Mary have lived at or near St. Louis, with the subscriber, for about 15 years. It is supposed that they are making their way to Chicago, and that a white man accompanies them, that they will travel chiefly at night, and most probably in a covered wagon.

A reward of $150 will be paid for their apprehension, so that I can get them, if taken within one hundred miles of St. Louis, and $200 if taken beyond that, and secured so that I can get them, and other reasonable additional charges, if delivered to the subscriber, or to THOMAS ALLEN, Esq., at St. Louis, Mo. The above negroes, for the last few years, have been in possession of Thomas Allen, Esq., of St. Louis.
Wm. Russell
St. Louis, Oct. 1, 1847

ALBERT A. BELL, JR, discovered his love of writing in high school, and his writing was first published in 1972. Although he considers himself a "shy person," he also describes himself more as a storyteller than a literary artist. He says, "When I read a book, I am more interested in one with a plot that keeps moving than long descriptive passages or philosophical reflection." He writes books he would enjoy reading himself.

Dr. Bell has taught at Hope College in Holland, Michigan since 1978; and, from 1994-2004, served as Chair of the History Department. He holds a Ph.D. from UNC-Chapel Hill, and is married to psychologist Bettye Jo Barnes Bell. They have four children and a grandson.

Bell's published works include contemporary mysteries: *Death Goes Dutch* and *Kill her Again*; and, in the historical vein, *All Roads Lead to Murder*, and *Daughter of Lazarus*. His nonfiction works include *Perfect Game, Imperfect Lives, Exploring the New Testament*, and, co-authored with James B. Allis, *Resources in Ancient Philosophy*. His articles have appeared in a wide variety of publications, such as *Jack and Jill, True Experience*, and *Detroit Free Press* and *Christian Century*.